Auntie Lizzie's Bedroom Floor

A story book for children

by Phil Gowler

Auntie Lizzie's Bedroom Floor

ISBN-13: 978-1517171780
ISBN-10: 1517171784

Published by Amazon
Book design by Chrystel Melhuish
www.plumdesignpublishing.com

Illustrations by Jonarton
www.jonarton.com

Dedications

This book is dedicated to two of my daughters, Claire and Liz. These two young ladies between them managed to achieve a mess in their bedrooms that has never been equalled.

Imagine if you will, a ghetto slum that has been trampled by an enraged herd of angry flatulent elephants suffering from severe food poisoning, rolled up by a fleet of bulldozers, had a large municipal tip mixed in and then lived in for a couple of centuries by giant cockroaches engaged in permanent warfare with giant dung beetles, both sides using intercontinental nuclear poo missiles.

Not forgetting of course my other daughter Rebecca and her two inspiring grandchildren Erin and Ethan.

Finally my long suffering wife Julie, who has put up with all my follies, daydreams and silliness since before time began...

Thank you

I would like to thank Chrystel Melhuish for her book design and constant support once I decided to get on with this project and Jon the illustrator who has done an amazing job for me.

And the late and much missed Terry Pratchett, who inspired me to start this book some years ago.

In the beginning…

It was just a normal house spider, quite small, but with those long hairy legs that still meant is was capable of sending ladies running screaming from the room in search of the bleach bottle, or a slipper. As such, it had a mind, but it was just focused on the stuff a small brain would focus on- food, survival, and making baby spiders. Making ladies scream was just a pleasant side effect of having eight hairy legs.

It wasn't a big spider, and so had been chased around by much larger ones, and if it was possible for such a creature to harbour a grudge, then it was certainly starting to get peeved.

Right now it had taken refuge under a huge, soft springy thing that one of the resident ladies used to lie on at night.
(I wonder how many of you realise that itchy nose feeling you get when you are asleep is because the spiders come out, climb onto your nose, and make faces at you. Nothing at all to worry about.)

But this evening, this particular spider was tired and fed up, and very hungry. So it crawled under the mattress (for that is what the huge springy thing was) fully resigned to the fact that it would just have to ignore its hunger for today and fall asleep.

Except that something made its head prick up, and the hairs on its legs stand on end. In the darkness ahead of it, it sensed a dark shape, much bigger than it was. It smelled like food. However, the spider also sensed a vague whispering voice in its mind, a soft voice that spoke of power and dark revenge, promising domination and control.

So it approached cautiously, legs waving out in front until they brushed against a strange material. It knew from experience that it was the kind of material humans made and sometimes kept food inside.

Yet it also sensed that inside that material was the mind that it had felt, and it was stronger now, coiling and moving, whispering the temptation of ultimate power, not just over other spiders, but bleach-wielding humans too.

It poked a careful foot at the material, which surprisingly gave way, and suddenly a sticky black liquid surge burst out, grabbed the surprised and helpless spider and sucked it inside.

You would have thought that was it. Slightly weird, but one spider less is neither here nor there.

Except... The spider woke up.

Erin loved going to see her grandparents. Well, in truth, so did her brother Ethan. She loved her own house, it was very small and great fun to live in, and being small it meant that it was almost like a rather large play house, choc full of toys of all kinds. Despite the fact that she was only six, a family full of doting relatives had already supplied her with a selection of playthings that was (almost) impossible to choose from.

You may be surprised that this adventure happened to a seven year old girl. Well, to start with, it is well known that girls are smarter than boys. Being younger than Ethan she had learned to fight for attention, and being 'too big for her boots' as her mummy would say, which meant that although she was only seven, she had the wisdom and piercing perspicacity of an old granny, and the sheer vindictiveness of a Sicilian bandit.

She loved sharing her room with Ethan. He was older than her, but despite that, he allowed her to boss him around, steal his toys and stand on his foot. Being brother and sister they always seemed to be on the verge of fighting or playing and one little thing could tip them one way or the other.

Her mother Rebecca was the eternal referee in this never-ending conflict. At first she used to dash in at the sound of screams, separate the warring pair and make some attempt at listening to their stories of who did what to whom. After a year or two of that, she had developed the much more pragmatic solution of letting the conflict evolve, knowing that sooner or later one would win, the other sulk and eventually both would forget it and things return back to normal.

Every now and again, Erin and Ethan would go to see their grandparents. This was a real treat for them to look forward to. A different house, new things to explore, new ways to get into trouble and a lovely big garden populated with brightly coloured fish in their own pond, bugs and crawly things in the wildlife pond, birds in the trees and a multitude of insects.

There were trees to be climbed, rocks to be clambered over, compost heaps to be poked into, vegetables to be picked for lunch, stones to fall over and sharp garden tools to play with, amongst an enormous selection of various objects, plants, garden sprays, hoses and many other things to pick up and get told off for.

But every now and again, the kids would have to go inside, when it was raining ('what's wrong with getting wet?'), or when they had lunch to eat ('boring!'), or when they had to go to the loo.

Now the bathroom could be a fun place too, and Erin would reach up and lock the door, knowing her mummy would panic because she could be playing with grandpa's razors, or eating the soap (eewww nasty), or just sitting on the toilet, swinging her legs in the air and thinking about life and the world.

Next to the bathroom was Auntie Lizzie's bedroom. Erin could get into grandpa's and grandma's bedroom. Lots of fun to be had there, ornaments to play with ('Erin! put that down now!'), odd things in the bedside cabinets ('Oh my god have you seen what she has got now?'), and a lovely big bed to hide in and play peek-a-boo with grandpa when he was pretending to be a big scary dog. Of course, the aim of being the big scary dog was to get her out of the room and away from all the breakables, but it never quite worked out that way.

Auntie Lizzie's bedroom though was a mystery. Somehow, whenever she and her brother visited, the door was always locked. It was just a normal door, big and white, with a red surround, a few scratches and dirty marks on it, but never, ever open. Both Erin and Ethan were fascinated by it; after all, it is quite human to be curious about a locked door. But no matter how hard they pushed on it, or rattled the handle, it was always resolutely closed.

Until one oddly eventful day that would change Erin's life forever.

It was a usual Sunday morning, Erin and Ethan were arguing over toys. Ethan was getting slightly the better of the argument as he was hitting her repeatedly over the head with a large toy car while she was trying to reach it and screaming at the top of her voice.

In the background, the phone started to ring which instantly stopped the pair of them in their tracks and they dashed over to the phone that was on the small table by the window. They weren't fast enough however as their mum zoomed out of the kitchen and grabbed the phone first. When you are a mother of young children you learn to move fast.

It was Grandma on the phone, which the kids instantly realised, and started jumping up and down, pleading to talk to her.

'In a minute' their mum said crossly, trying to shoo them away.

They could tell that the phone call was about coming over to visit, so they got more excited, jumping up and down and screeching to be heard. 'Ok,' their mum said into the phone, 'You can pick us up at 11'. Then she added: 'Do you want to speak to the kids?'

That was a bit of an unnecessary question, Grandma always wanted to talk to the kids. Getting to speak first you would think would be Ethan's choice, as he was the eldest by a couple of years. But as her mum started to pass the phone to Ethan, Erin dashed in and grabbed it, and running like a hare she shot under the table with the phone knowing that she could squeeze into a corner behind the chairs where Ethan couldn't reach her. He did indeed chase after her, but in vain, and had to watch in frustration as she poked her tongue out at him and spoke on the phone.

'Hello Grandma' she said into the receiver, and she heard grandma's distant voice reply -

'Hello Erin, how are you sweeties?'

'Ethan hurt me' she replied.

'Oh dear' sympathised Grandma, 'what did he do?'

'He pinched me' replied Erin.

'That's not true!' Ethan shouted.

Granny heard this and asked:

'Are you lying Erin?'

'Yes' she replied cheerfully. After all, she is an honest little girl. Some of the time.

Phone calls with small children do require a certain amount of patience. So Grandma patiently sat through the list of largely fictitious injuries inflicted on Erin by her brother, what she had for breakfast, what she was wearing, where she went one day last week, where mummy was, and the interesting stain on her white shoe that looked like 'Yucky dog poo Grandma!'

Eventually she crawled out from between the chair legs and gave up the phone to Ethan, and Grandma again had a list of Ethan's injuries to listen to (real ones, Erin packs a hard right hook), what he had done at school, what he wanted for lunch and even a Christmas request for a train set. It was August, but Ethan did like to plan ahead.

So now for the next couple of hours the children fussed over what to wear (Erin was easy to dress, anything pink would do usually, although today she opted for a dark green kilt), what to take, what sweets and snacks to bring, and new toys to show off to their grandparents. Their mum was fussing too, making sure that they had spare clothes for when Ethan discovered how to turn on the garden tap while the hose was attached, and for when Erin decided to go newt hunting in the pond. Secretly she was hoping that Grandpa had a spare glass or two of wine she could have, children can easily drive you to drink!

Later that day Grandma arrived in her big blue car. The car was called Hyacinth, twenty years ago it had probably been owned by someone called Hyacinth, who sat in the back seat while her husband chauffeured her to church and the local shops. Now it was just a big, rather grand and slightly battered old car. The kids loved it because it had electric windows ('Erin, wind that window up now!'), and an electric sunroof ('Erin, sit down and get your head out of that sun roof!'). Ethan rather liked the horn, and while Erin was being strapped into her seat, he would sit in the front, turning the steering wheel and beeping the horn.

The kids loved their Grandma of course. She was a short and dare I say it- round little lady, with a face rather like a sweet but slightly wrinkly apple. Usually she had a fag hanging out of her mouth and lager bottle never too far away, with a huge smile and always ready to laugh.

Grandma's laugh was legendary; when she got the laughing fit she would go bright red and laugh until the tears ran down her face. She had a job that the kids thought was perfect - she worked in a cake shop. That meant cakes for all if they went into town to see her, even if mummy did disapprove a little.

They loved Grandpa too of course. But he was different. They loved rubbing his bushy beard, they would scream with laughter as they bounced on his belly, or dived on him from the sofa. But when he did his big scary bear impression, their screams of laughter could easily become screams of fear, Grandpa was very strong and would throw them into the air like rag dolls or turn them upside down in a trice, laughing in his big, deep voice as they shouted for mercy. Sometimes there would be tears, but soon forgotten once they started jumping on him again, or prodding his belly and running away calling him 'Mister Stinky'. Grandpa's one amazing skill as far as they were concerned was making fart noises (or even real farts). It never failed to reduce them to tears of laughter.

But let us get back to the story. This was a lovely sunny day, so the adults were all sitting outside. Erin and Ethan were not sitting of course; they were poking things they shouldn't, investigating where they weren't allowed to go, and generally needing watching with both eyes.

Erin realised she needed to go to the little girl's room, so she ran back towards the house.

'Where are you going Erin?' shouted her mum.

'Just to the toilet mummy' she shouted over her shoulder, and ran through the house and up the stairs to the bathroom. Right next to the bathroom was Auntie Lizzie's bedroom door, which was never open.

But strangely enough, as she pushed the bathroom door open, she heard a very slight creaking noise. Turning, she noticed that the door that was never open was in fact ever so slightly open, just a tiny, tiny bit. Toilet forgotten, she stepped quietly over to the door and pushed it inwards.

As the door opened, at first all she could see was darkness. The curtains inside the room were obviously closed and visible in the distance only by the fact that they were a slightly grey shape rather than blackness. She stood in the doorway, letting her eyes get used to the gloom. Normally, she would be the first to dash towards something new, but the room was so dark and quiet that it was scary. She seemed to feel that there were a lot of objects in the room and the floor looked much jumbled.

Her nose wrinkled a little as well, the room had an odd smell, sort of sour and dusty, a bit like an old dustbin. Last year, at the end of the summer holidays, she had dug her school bag out from under the bed, and on opening it had found a very brown, wrinkled and squishy banana at the bottom, it smelt pretty much the same as the room did now.

After a few minutes, the gloom seemed to subside a little and she could see a lot of mess and undefined clutter of vague shapes on the floor, a bed up against the far wall and a bookcase next to her just by the door. Somewhere near the bed she sort of guessed that the dark looming shape there was a cupboard, or chest of drawers. Everything seemed to be covered in a haphazard pile of old clothes, food wrappers and just general mess. Erin froze for a second as she felt she saw something move on the floor, somewhere in the gloom.
But her curiosity got the better of her, deciding to go in and explore, she took a step into the room, reaching her hand out to the bookcase just to steady herself. As she did so, she felt a sudden tiny but sharp pain in the palm of her hand as it touched the bookcase. She snatched it back, mouth open about to shout or cry. But nothing came out, and suddenly she felt very weird, the room seemed to swirl in her head, her legs felt like they were jelly and she fell to her knees, then finally slipped to the ground and everything went black.

Who knows what happened then, or how long she was there, it could have been a second or hours. But when she woke up and found herself sitting on the floor, she felt sort of....different. She could still see the grey shape of the window, but it now seemed impossibly small and high above her and so far away.

In the distance loomed the shape of the bed, but that too seemed high and very far away. Somehow she sensed that the room had become vast, a giant dark and frightening cave, and it was silent. There was no sound from outside, no noise of cars on the road, just stillness as if the world was holding its breath and unseen eyes were upon her.

And even as she gazed upwards, the shape of the window seemed to be moving away from her and the darkness grew, multiplying the terror that she felt swelling inside her. Close to her, in a sort of middle distance, there were jumbled shapes that could have been distant mountains, or just odd patches of darkness, to her right and in front of her, the shapes began to look almost like huge, dark tower blocks, sombre and silent. What was strangest of all though, was the way she felt.

'I feel different' she said hesitantly in a quavering voice and clapped her hands over her mouth, because her voice was indeed not the same, it had somehow deepened a little. Thoughts were coming into her head, and words, words that she didn't know she knew. She struggled to express what she was thinking, and all of a sudden it came to her. 'I feel older' she whispered.

This was odd, very odd, but somehow although it was scaring her, it was sort of fascinating as well. Children can sometimes adapt to frightening situations better than adults. Grown-ups know all the awful things that may happen and children don't, they haven't been around long enough to know all the bad things that can happen, so they can cope with things that adults may not be able to.

She had a weird feeling that inside her head a little girl was crying for her mummy, but a bigger girl had temporarily at least taken control and was determined not to cry, and although she was scared, she wanted to find out what was going on.

So she stood up. She looked down at herself and her clothes seemed to be the same. It did appear to be getting a little lighter in the room; either that or her eyes were getting accustomed to the gloom. As she looked down, she noticed the ground was hard and blue, and seemed to be made of tightly woven fabric that was springy and hairy. Bending down, she rubbed her hand over the prickly surface.

'It's carpet' she said to herself, and added: 'I'm still in Auntie Lizzie's room.' But as she looked round, she also whispered: 'But why is everything so big?'

And indeed it was. For now she realised that the huge shapes in front of her and to the left were in fact jumbled mountains of old clothes, towering above like huge musty mountains. The floor stretched a little way in front of her, but somewhere in the middle distance to the right of the clothes mountains, she could just about make out a sort of white fluffy cloud that appeared to be hugging the ground.

Further away to the right and in the distance, she realised that the giant tower blocks were the bookcase and the chest of drawers. And in the far distance behind the clothes mountains and the white fluffy cloud, was in fact the bed, huge and impossibly tall.

All over the furniture and scattered across the floor, she could see all kinds of weird shapes that looked like giant toys and huge, towering ornaments, twisted shapes distorted by distance and perspective. Her eyes felt a bit like a zoom lens on a camera, focusing in and out and trying to get her brain to make sense of it all.

Imagine a primitive man, minding his own business in the dim and distant past. There he is, hairy and brutish, trying to hit fish in a river with his club. Then there is an odd noise, a large blue box suddenly appears and a strange skinny man with spiky hair dashes out of the blue box, drags our ape-man inside and then seconds later deposits him in the middle of modern day New York. Before he has time to grunt 'Hey, that box is bigger on the inside!' his eyes make the connection to his brain, which explodes as it overloaded with sights, sound and strangeness.

Taking all this in, her first and most sensible instinct was to turn around and head for the doorway. It was some distance away, but even as she reached it she saw that the giant white door was firmly closed. Small as she was, there was no way she could squeeze under it, much less open it.

It was around about now that the little girl inside her finally got her way and she sat down heavily, tears beginning to roll silently down her face. After all, when you are little you can be very grown up and sensible for a while, but sooner or later the child inside you will come out. She was totally confused and completely at a loss to understand what was happening.

So she sat there and the tears rolled down her face. But quite soon, she stopped crying, because she could hear something odd in the distance, a weird sort of metallic boinggggg noise, which was getting closer. Standing up, she looked in the direction the noise was coming from. It was definitely getting a bit lighter now, and so she quickly spotted a shape that was bouncing towards her. 'Jack-in-a-box?' she thought.

But no, it was too hairy, and seemed to have big shapeless clothes that were flying up in the air every time it bounced. So she reasoned it wasn't a kangaroo either. However the weird clothes and flying hair were a little scary, and she could just make out that it looked like a man with an impossibly wide grin. The grin didn't help though, it was not reassuring.

'Oh my!' she exclaimed, 'It's a clown!' and at that thought she instantly wanted somewhere to hide, even though the clown was obviously heading for her. But it was too late, the clown had obviously seen her.

'Allo leetle girl!' it called, and then added: 'Do not be afred, I am not going to hurt vous.'

So poor Erin stood still, watching the clown as it bounced closer. Now she realised why it was bouncing, it seemed to have the top half of a clown, but its bottom half was a large, slightly bent spring attached to a wooden base.

His coat was brightly striped, with many colours and it was obviously way too large, which is why it was flying in the air at every leap upwards. Indeed as he bounced up, the coat would fly up so far, it covered his head, revealing a sort of white stringy vest underneath. Then there would be a slight pause at the top of his bounce before he descended. As he came down, his huge shock of orange hair would hang in the air for a second, looking as if he had a set of pointy horns. When he hit the ground, his face would scrunch up, making him look like a bulldog with a painted face, and as he bounced up, his mouth came open and his tongue would flop out and wave around. He looked quite ridiculous, and Erin forgot her fear, and found she was wondering if he would bite his tongue off by accident. He was now waving his arms at her as he got closer.

‘Do not paneek leetle one’ he shouted. ‘I will be weeth you momentarily’, and indeed he was now very close.

Erm...too close. Even though Erin was little, she realised as he got closer that unless he could stop dead, he was either going to bounce over her, or land right on her. As if sensing this, the clown shouted again: ‘Eet is ok; I can stop anytime I want.’

True to his word, as he got a few feet away from her he came to a sudden stop. Unfortunately, he seemed to have taken no account of the laws of motion. Coming to a sudden stop meant that his spring still wanted to go forward. Which it did.

Erin had to suddenly jump backwards as the spring bent forward and whacked the clown’s forehead on the floor, then obeying another law of physics, it shot backwards and thumped the back of the clown’s head on the floor behind him.

‘Ow...sheet, bugger...’ exclaimed the clown in pain and embarrassment, for the backward momentum propelled the spring forward again, and once more the front of his head smacked into the ground in front of her and shot backwards.

'Eet is ok' he exclaimed as he bounced from one thump to another. 'Eet will stop in a minute, and I have a wooden head, so I am ok.'

Erin couldn't resist a giggle at this point, and indeed the violent swinging back and forth slowed, until the clown was swaying gently on his spring in front of her.

His eyes were rolling a little and he put his hands to the side of his head, as if to get his bearings. Finally, he looked as if everything had settled down and he looked at her. And smiled. Not a scary clown smile, just a big friendly one. He extended a white gloved hand.

'Allow me to introduce myself,' he said as Erin gingerly shook his hand. 'I have the honour to be Stephane, I am ze Springy clown. And who are you?' he asked.

'I am Erin' she replied, and then added, 'why are you talking funny?
He looked puzzled.

'Funny, moi?' he wondered. Then he realised what she meant. 'Ah!' he exclaimed pointing a stiff, white-gloved finger in the air, 'I am French, you silly girl, thees is not talking funny, it is just my accent you know.'

'What does 'French' mean?' Erin asked.

'Incroyable!' Stephane exclaimed. 'You eenglish are so stupide. I come from France of course, ma petit imbecile. I am here because your stupide auntie bought me at a fair years ago, and then left me in thees room full of... Well, what can I say?'

'Oh' Erin replied. 'But I am not stupid you know, we haven't done French at school yet.'
The clown seemed a little mollified by this and he reached down and ruffled her hair.

'Do not worry, mon enfant, I could never be angry with a petit fille like yourself.'

Ruffling a girl's hair is not a good thing to do; it takes ages to get it looking right. But Erin was in a forgiving mood as despite the weirdness of this situation, she was fascinated by the bobbing clown and of course quite worried about what on earth was happening.

Stephane leaned forward and this time looked at her seriously. ‘I bet you are worried what on earth is happening’ he said. She nodded, and also noticed that his accent seemed to have disappeared.

‘It’s like this’, he went on, ‘Somehow, you have got in here from the Outside.’ As if anticipating her question he continued, ‘It is hard to explain, but just underneath the world you know, where you can’t see it, even though it’s there, is another world. Both worlds live inside each other, which is impossible, but nevertheless true. And rarely, usually by accident, people -or things, (he added sombrely) can travel between these worlds, or get pushed....or fall’

He stopped here. Erin was looking very thoughtful as she digested this. Then she looked up at the clown and asked:

‘So my toys come alive?’

'Yes,' Stephane replied, 'I suppose so, but you will never see it in your world, only in this one.' This only served to increase the frown on Erin's face as she struggled with this. With some degree of thought, she added slowly,

'So... in my bedroom, my toys are all lying around waiting for me play with them, while *at the same time* in this world they are all running around and doing things that I can't see.'

Stephane nodded which is not a good idea for a springy clown, because it set him swaying forwards and backwards again, much to her amusement. When his swaying had subsided a little, he looked down at her and remarked,

'I bet you are thinking it would be lovely to play with all your dolls as real people, aren't you?' Erin nodded.

'But,' added the clown, 'the toy dinosaurs are real, the soldiers, the spacemen, the monsters, and just imagine all the toys out there with no heads, or arms, or legs, all coming alive.' He shuddered. 'It's my world, but sometimes it even scares me.'

He had a point and Erin silently digested the thought. Then she asked the obvious question.

'Why am I here?'

Now it was the turn of the clown to look thoughtful.

'I don't know' he said, 'but I fear it was no accident. And if you want to get back to your world, I would say that it is impossible. But I have heard a rumour that some kind of door has recently appeared, right in the corner of the wall, under the bed. Those of us that live here can't use it, we just seem to walk into the wall, but apparently someone has come through it to our world.'

'Let's go then' said Erin brightly, for despite the momentary fun of having a bouncy clown as a friend, she was already missing her brother and family. Stephane leaned even closer to her this time without swaying at all, and looked her right in the eyes.

'Ma pauvre petite, it will be very dangerous, there are many bad things here. Your Auntie Lizzie has a very bad room; there are things that live here that you do not want to meet.'

'What else can I do?' she responded. 'I have to get home somehow.'

'You are right of course' replied Stephane. 'But there are some places I cannot go, at least not on my own.'
He paused in thought for a moment, and look at her as if he was weighing her up somehow.

'If you are brave and can wait for me' he mused, 'I can go and get a friend who can help you, and you will be safer. Can you wait here for a little while? You will have to be very strong and try not to get frightened.'

He paused again, still looking intently at her. Then he turned to his right and pointed. 'Do you see those hills of old clothes over there?' he asked. She peered into the gloom.

'Yes' she replied.

'We call them the Musty Mountains. If you get worried, run over there and find somewhere to hide, I am sure you will be able to see me when I come back.'

Erin paused nervously, but she really had no choice and reluctantly agreed. Stephane bounced off with a wave of his hand in farewell.

‘Do not worry’ he shouted in farewell, ‘I will be back soon’, and she watched him as he bounced off into the distance, hair and coat flying in the air as he went up and down.

So Erin was left all alone, standing on the wide expanse of carpet and looking around her. Once Stephane was out of sight, it went very quiet. It was quite strange that in a room in a house in a normal street she couldn't hear any of the usual noises that you would expect to hear.

But it was silent and quite eerie. In fact the more she thought about it, the spookier it got, here she was in supposedly another world that was wrapped around her own, all alone and totally dependent on a French clown and some kind of 'magic' doorway that was under the bed and seemingly miles away.

Then she thought of all the things you get under the bed. Broken toys, dirt, dust, beetles, ants, dead flies.
Spiders.
Oh dear, spiders. And they would be spiders at her size, giant, scary and hungry.
Oh dear, oh dear.
Spiders.

Erin literally had to shake herself to stop thinking about spiders. After all, Stephane had promised a friend to help, and there must be other nice friends out there too. She tried to persuade herself that Auntie Lizzie was a girl too, so she must have dollies and teddy bears and fluffy lovely toys of all kinds.

Then it occurred to her that you don't actually KNOW if your toys were nice. After all, they could be evil for all you know.
And *then* came another thought as she remembered all the toys she had trod on, thrown against the wall, hit Ethan on the head with, broken, lost and generally abused.
Oh dear, oh dear.
And spiders...

So she sat down, and decided to be as quiet and unobtrusive as she could. She even tried not to make a noise breathing, but very soon realised she did have to breathe, although you could do it quietly.

She also noticed that there were indeed noises in the background, but they were very faint and very soft. Maybe she was imagining it, but some of the sounds were like small rain drops landing on soft grass... or... tiny legs running swiftly over carpet...

'Don't be silly!' she chided herself, and huddled down even tighter.

To her relief though, it wasn't too long before she could hear a familiar boinging noise and in the distance she saw Stephane bouncing as ridiculously as ever as he got closer.

He was obviously pleased to see her because he was waving his arms and shouting. He seemed to have brought several friends; she could see vague, moving shapes running swiftly behind him.

But as he got closer, she started to worry. His waving was a little too frantic, his bouncing was a little too fast and the friends following him seemed rather to be chasing him rather than following.

There was something sort of familiar about them too, something that seemed to activate a deep internal rush of fear, they were squat and low to the ground, but moving very quickly.

Then, a bit like one of those magic pictures that look like a jumble of coloured dots before they suddenly seem to re-arrange themselves into a picture of a dinosaur; everything became clear.

Stephane was waving frantically and the word he was shouting was:
'Spiders!'

Heart beating wildly, she jumped up, but then instinctively bent low, perhaps hoping that they wouldn't see her. She looked around frantically and made the instant decision to head for the mountain of dirty clothing to her left.

She shot off, behind her she could still hear Stephane shouting and the 'thunk!' every time he bounced. Was it getting nearer? She wasn't sure and she daren't look back.

The clothing mountain loomed over her, but it didn't indeed seem to be getting any nearer, and the sound of pursuit seemed closer. She started to imagine she could hear the swift patter of spider feet, and terror leant her new energy and she sped forward, finally reaching a huge out-flung sleeve. Scrambling on top, the fabric yielded slightly to her feet, but she was able to keep running and climbing, clambering over folds, sliding down the other side and heading ever upwards. In front of her, she saw an opening next to a large button and she dived for it, falling slightly as the fabric moved and closed over her slightly, leaving her in a dark, warm and slightly smelly space.

She was gasping for breath, but trying hard not to gasp loudly. Outside she could hear something, but the clothes muffled the sound, and she daren't move. She even pressed her face against the rough material, nose wrinkling a little at the slightly rancid smell, but terrified all the same that someone or something would hear her. As her eyes got used to the darkness in her hiding place, she realised that she was trapped in here, the fabric didn't appear to have any creases or folds she could crawl further into.

However Erin was a brave girl. After all, this was the little girl who would jump off anything, chase anything, and pick up anything. Once her breathing had calmed a little, she risked it and crawled as slowly and as very quietly as she could up to the opening and very, very slowly poked her head out.

She noticed in some surprise that she had climbed further than she expected, and she could see the floor where she had been. But there was an awful sight to see on there, because Stephane was standing there, swaying slightly, and stalking around him were three huge, hairy, and very nasty looking spiders. Each one was as a big as a large dog, black all over with bristling short, harsh hairs. But it was their heads that scared her, they had bulging multiple eyes, and fangs that snapped as they talked and dripped a dark green venom.

They were circling the clown, who was looking quickly and nervously around him, shaking and swaying, licking his dry lips in fear. Erin looked on at the scene, frozen in fear herself, trying almost to stop breathing. She didn't really know if the spiders were bad, or would hurt her, but there is something about a spider, all those legs, the fangs, the horrid eyes.

Plus of course the fact that they sting you so you are paralysed, then slowly suck the juice from the victim's body while they are still alive.

Apart from Stephane's heavy breathing, all she could hear was the soft patter of all the spiders feet as they circled the clown. But then, to make the scene more horrible they began to speak in a soft, hissing voice.

'Sssoooo' whispered one. 'It is the sad little bouncing clown, what are you doing out here, all alone?'

'P-P-Please' stammered Stephane, 'I was doing nothing, just going to visit the Dolly Sisters'. At this, all the spiders hissed together.

'Sssssisterssssss', they hissed, it seemed to be a word they didn't like, for their circling of the clown speeded up, and became more agitated.

'Where issss the girl?' hissed another spider. Stephane stammered again.

'G-G-Girl?' he asked. 'I don't know any girls, except for the Sisters I suppose.' The spiders all hissed again.

'Tell usssss' they breathed, 'or you will die.' Stephane held his hands out in supplication,

'I don't know any girl, please let me go.'
As if in answer to this, the spiders speeded up their circling of the clown, who kept twisting his head round and round, trying to keep them all in sight at the same time.

Suddenly one leaped right over the clown's head, who ducked, but he could not avoid the thin trailing web that draped across him. He pawed at it, but the strand seemed to stick to his fingers. The other spiders all followed suit, leaping over him and running round him, spinning their webs around and around him until he was totally covered in ropes of spider web, except for his head.

Finally the spiders, leaving their strands attached to their bodies, used them as ropes and hauled the hapless clown away. As they disappeared, Erin could hear his voice pleading, but the spiders were paying no attention and off they went into the darkness.

Now, as we saw a little while ago, when Erin changed and fell into this strange world, she seemed to have become different, almost older, or shall we say, less childish. You would think at this point she would be screaming, or crying at the sight of giant spiders dragging off a talking clown toy. But she wasn't. Oh, she was scared alright, her heart was pounding and she had never felt so frightened, but somehow, deep down, she felt that she had to stay in control. However unreal this place was, it was real to her and she had to stay in control if she was to make any sense of things and get back home.

So, taking a bit of a deep breath, she started to think about what she could do next. Remembering the words of the clown, she realised that her best way out was some kind of doorway under the bed. Not a happy thought really. But the mountainous piles of clothing in which she found herself seemed to be a good way, if difficult. She had no wish to cross the open space of the floor where a sudden attack by swift spiders would give her nowhere to run, and she was pretty certain that they would run much faster than her.

So, checking carefully around her, she emerged slowly from her warm hole and started to climb upwards. It was difficult to see far into the distance, but she had a rough idea of where she was heading, and sort of guessed that the clothes mountain would end at the bed.

The big advantage to climbing a clothes mountain, is that there aren't really any sheer slopes to climb, and if you fall, there is at least a soft landing. But she found that the climb was very tiring. Her footing was at times very soft and so her feet would sink down, it was almost like trying to walk in sand or mud.

Also, there was the smell. Or maybe better to say, the Smell. It gradually seemed to insinuate itself into her nose and she felt that she was breathing it in and it was coating her lungs with a sort of sticky dampness. It was a vague mix of sourness and damp. Not a strong smell, but already she seemed to be soaked in it, it was on her skin, in her clothes, and gradually became almost unbearable.

She also found that she had to be careful where she was treading. Interspersed amongst the relatively firm footholds offered by dirty jeans or old jumpers, there was the much more dangerous footing of shiny, silky fabrics, which, as she found, were almost like walking on ice. They were very slippery, and hard to hold on to.

And although it would be unlikely she would fall to her death, there were deep, dark valleys to be avoided, or sudden crevasses. If she fell into them, she would face a long and exhausting climb upwards, and that doesn't even include all the nasty creepy things that might be waiting for her at the bottom. Her imagination had already started to run a little wild, after all, there are more things than spiders in a room. Flies... giant flies eating their own vomit... woodlice with all those hairy tickly legs... wasps... ants...

So she gave a little shudder and tried to block all these thoughts from her mind and concentrate on what she had to do.

So, onwards and upwards she climbed. It was so difficult, her feet were sinking into the soft fabric as she lifted them up, her hands gripping the fabric had begun to ache, and she knew she was feeling hungry now and thirsty. That climb seemed endless, and was done largely in silence, so was eerie and dream-like. Every time she scrambled and pulled herself up onto a soft, slightly sagging ledge, there was more mountain towering above her. Not to mention the Smell, which was starting to cling to her like a teenager's trainers.

She did finally get herself onto a high ledge and decided it was a good place for a rest. There was indeed more clothing piled above her, but as she sat down, she could see that she had come a long way. Below her were the valleys and slopes she had clambered up, in the far distance was the darkness of the open floor. Way in the remote distance, she could almost make out the half-guessed looming shape of the bookcase shelves, towering high above everything.

'I must be nearly there' she said to herself, and was conscious of the dryness of her lips and the rumbling of hunger in her stomach.

Then, she thought she noticed some movement, just below her to the left. She peered down anxiously, and saw that it looked more like a small earthquake, the ground, or rather the clothes, appeared to be moving, but not randomly. It was as if something was burrowing under the surface, and she noticed with some dismay that the movements appeared to be coming towards her. Jumping to her feet, her one thought was to climb upwards, despite her tiredness.

But it seemed she was too late, for behind her there was a soft rumbling noise and a sort of slithering sound. Turning round, she screamed as an impossibly huge snake-like creature erupted from the mountainside and towered over her. It was striped in many colours, but she didn't notice them much, what was much more concerning was the enormous, dark, wide open mouth that was heading towards her, and, transfixed by fear, the giant snake grasped her in its mouth, lifted her up, and swallowed her whole.

Now usually in books like this, the author will say something like “all went black, and she fainted. When she awoke...” Well, Erin is not the fainting type. She was tired, thirsty, scared and very angry. So as she fell into the warm and surprising woolly gullet, she started to kick out and punch the yielding walls.

'Let me out! Let me out!' she screamed, as she kicked and punched. Sure enough, she felt herself rise as if the monster snake was itself rearing up in the air, and then there was a convulsion in the mouth and she flew through the air, arms and legs flailing wildly, landing on the ledge she had just been grabbed from.

She lay there for a second, getting her thoughts together, and wondering if she would have to get up and run. She sat up, and there, right in front of her, the multicoloured snake was resting its head on the ground, and she was looking into its bold, shiny eyes, stuck on either side of its head, like giant black beads. It wasn't doing anything much, except lying there and looking at her, wide mouth firmly closed. Rather disconcertingly the black shiny eyes didn't blink.

She didn't quite know what to do next as they both looked at each other. So she did what she did best and wagged her finger at it.

'Bad snake' she said, and the snake's brow puckered a little, making it look almost humble and it shrank back a little. Then it spoke, in a soft, deep rumble of a voice.

'I'm sorry', it said sadly. 'I wouldn't have eaten you; I mistook you for something else.'

Oh well, thought Erin, talking clowns, talking spiders and now giant, multicoloured talking snakes. Why am I surprised?

Out loud she asked defiantly,

'Mistook me for what?'

'A sock of course' rumbled the snake, and added 'I eat socks'.

'Eat socks?' Erin asked quizzically, and then added 'that's stupid'. The snake smiled, its woolly mouth bending upwards into a big grin.

'Is it?' he rumbled. 'I wonder how many odd socks you have. I wonder why you can never find the missing one?'

This gave Erin pause for thought. It was certainly true that socks did go missing, and for no apparent reason. No amount of searching would find them, and the odd sock would get thrown in the odd sock bag, in the forlorn hope that one day a pair could be reunited and worn again.

While she was thinking, the giant sock-eating snake said: 'My name is Handy.' Erin thought for a minute and her reply shows just how special a little girl she was.

'Handy? Wouldn't that be a better name for a glove eating snake?' she asked. Handy thought about this for a second or so and said:

'Yes.'

Erin waited, expecting something else, but he didn't seem about to add anything, so she replied,

'My name is Erin' and extended her hand. Which Handy stared at, obviously not sure what to do.

'Good grief!' exclaimed Erin. 'You are called Handy and you don't even have any hands!'

'Sorry' replied Handy, and contrived somehow to look sad. So Erin patted him on the head instead, which he seemed to appreciate. 'Where are you going?' he asked.

Handy did seem to be a kindly, if slightly strange friend, so Erin told him everything that had happened to her, finishing with:

'I need to get under the bed and find a door out of here' she replied. Handy rumbled a little at that.

'It's dangerous under there.' he said, 'Not too dangerous for me, because I don't bother anyone, and they leave me alone, but it would be very dangerous for you.'

Erin looked despondent.

'I know.' she said in a quiet voice, 'And I'm scared, but what else can I do?'

They both paused in thought. After a moment or two, Handy rumbled again.

'Maybe the Dolly Sisters will know what can be done.'

'I've heard of them' Erin said, and then added in recollection, 'The spiders were talking about them when they dragged off poor Stephane.'

'Oh, they've caught Stephane have they?' Handy pondered and rumbled disapprovingly deep in his throat. Then he seemed to make a decision and moved closer to Erin, lifting his head slightly so it was level with hers, unwinking black orbs looking into her eyes. 'You must come with me to the Dolly Sisters', he said, adding 'They will explain everything, and they may be able to help.'

Erin's heart sank, for it seemed that getting away would not be easy.

'Is it far?' she asked.

'No, not all' he replied, and pointed upwards with his head. 'They are up there, on top of the flat wooden mountain.'

Erin looked up; Handy seemed to be pointing up at the cupboard that loomed darkly to one side of the mountains. It looked a long way away, and she wondered how she could get up to the top.

'It's so far' she sighed.

Handy laughed, a deep, rolling laugh.

'Not if you ride on the back of a sock eating monster it's not!' and Erin couldn't help but laugh too.

So Handy slid his way up to the ledge. He was very long and wide, with bright coloured stripes of all colours running around him in bands. Erin realised he was a giant sock, and then wondered why he would eat other socks, but didn't wonder for long. Apart from when he was eating her, Handy was obviously very friendly. She clambered across to just behind his head. He was indeed woolly and very easy to hold on to. She giggled a little, because his woolly skin tickled her legs.

'Hold on tight' he boomed, and off they went.
It was great fun sitting there, although a bit scary when she looked back and saw how high they were, but Handy seemed to know where he was going, and slid on, going up and up. He seemed to be able to glide over the deep crevasses that had scared her, and even take on steep slopes sideways, although that was very scary, as she clung on tightly she knew that there was nothing between her and the floor but a long drop. She

realised she had come a long way on foot, but there was still a long way to go, and it would have been very hard if she had walked and climbed the whole way.

As they went up, Handy turned slightly, so now the bed was to their right as he headed towards the cupboard. Erin felt that she was going away from where she needed to be, but the Dolly Sisters sounded like people she needed to meet, so she tried not to worry. It was hard not to cry when she thought of her family and how scared she was, but she remembered that sometimes when she was frightened her mummy had sung her a song to comfort her. So Erin leaned forward and asked Handy if he knew any songs they could sing. He didn't answer at first, so she suggested they sing one of her favourite songs, 'The Wheels On the Bus.'

'What's a wheel?' asked Handy.

'It's a round thing' she replied, 'Which the bus travels on. They have one at each corner.' Silly old snake she thought. There was a pause as Handy slithered on,

'What's a bus?' he asked.

Erin rolled her eyes, this was a little bit beyond her, anyway, she was now feeling tired. So tired in fact that she nestled against Handy's warm, woolly back, gripping tightly and fell asleep.

Some time later, she woke up, aware that they had stopped moving. 'Here we are.' rumbled Handy, and she saw the black cliff of the cupboard looming above them. They had reached the top of the clothes mountain, but here was another huge cliff to climb.

'How am I going to get up there?' she wondered out loud.

'Look over to your right' Handy suggested, and sure enough, she saw what looked like a rope hanging down from above. Sliding off Handy, she walked over to the rope and tugged at it. It certainly felt strong enough and safe enough.

But let us pause here a moment, after all, Erin is a little girl, climbing up a rope, hand over hand into the dark and unknown is hardly something that she could do, or probably even want to do. So the rope didn't seem to be much use.

Handy turned himself round and slid over to inspect the rope.

‘Tie it around your waist’ he suggested, ‘then pull hard on it three times.’
So she took the rope and wrapped it round and round her waist, also wrapping it around her arms and shoulders before pulling on it.
‘Three times.’ Handy reminded her, so she tugged it twice more. Suddenly the rope tightened around her waist and she began to rise in the air.

‘Goodbye Handy and thank you’ she cried.
In reply, Handy reared up to his full height before she disappeared into the darkness so she was able to stroke his head as she rose upwards.

‘Goodbye Little Sock.’ he replied. ‘I will wait here for you’, and she waved as she rose in the air, and kept waving until she couldn’t see him anymore.

Up she rose, up and up, bouncing gently off the wooden cupboard wall every now and again. The mountains were below her now, getting lost in the gloom, the very distant floor not really visible now.

The bed seemed closer now, off to one side and above the mountains, she could make out the top of the bed, a huge jumble of sheets and duvet that made it look like an icy white mountain range sitting at the top of the world.

It wasn't long before she sensed that she was getting close to the top. She had no idea, who was lifting her, but they seemed very strong. Looking up, she wasn't quite sure what she was seeing, a sort of giant, shiny figure that reflected some of the light that there was, and almost seemed transparent. It was obviously lifting her, but not with arms or hands or even fingers.

'Flippers?' she wondered.
And then, with a burst of speed, she had reached the top and was swung out onto the flat, dusty surface. Her guess was right, because, standing there was a giant glass penguin.
It was huge, it didn't just loom, it towered over her. She undid the rope from around herself, and the penguin silently coiled it up.

'Er, thanks.' said Erin. The penguin did not reply, although it did bow, a little stiffly. With a huge flipper, it pointed into the darkness.

‘I’m going that way then’ said Erin. The penguin pointed again. ‘Guess so. Oh well, thank you mister penguin’ she said and set off in the direction in which he had pointed.

‘I must stay away from the edge’ she said to herself, fearful of falling off into the depths. But the top of the cupboard wasn’t that big, so in a very short while she saw a large box in the distance. Well, it was a box normally, but at the height she was now it was as big as a house, so she thought maybe it could have been a house with no doors or windows, but a roof that opened instead.

What she could see though were three figures walking towards her. She knew straight away that they must be the Dolly Sisters, because although it was dark they looked just like china dolls, wearing frilly dresses, and lots and lots of lace.

The sister on the right was dressed in deep scarlet, and quite petite in stature, with short blonde hair and a very pretty face. The one in the middle was also quite petite, but with long dark hair, dressed in a short and very lacy black dress, with a pointy hat.

The one on the left was bigger and taller than the others, dressed in a large and long blue lace gown and wearing a huge hat with a feather in it. She was not only taller than the other two, but broader, and her dress and hat made her look a bit like a stately galleon in full sail.

'Good day young Erin' the middle sister said and took off her hat, revealing long curly dark hair. 'My name is Annie.' She indicated the sister on the right, the pretty blonde one. 'This is Yvonna.' Yvonna smiled at Erin, a bright, pink and pleasant smile. 'And this is Francesca', she said, indicating the remaining sister. Francesca smiled at her too.

'We know who you are of course', Francesca added.

'Hello' said Erin, trying to remember her manners, the sisters looked like they would expect politeness from a child. She felt the need to curtsey, so she did a shy little bob up and down.

'I bet you are hungry and thirsty.' observed Yvonna in a soft, lilting voice.

'Oh yes I am' Erin gasped. The sisters all smiled. Annie held out her hand, and Erin put her hand in hers.

'Let's see what we can find then.' said Annie kindly, and they all walked towards the box.

The 'box' was, like everything else around her, huge. It was black and shiny, but snaking across the black and shiny surface was a beautiful Chinese dragon, etched in gold and red, that glittered almost as if it was alive.

Francesca ran her hands across the carved dragon ornamentation, Erin thought that maybe she was pressing parts of the carving in a certain order, and the outline of a door appeared, that swung silently inwards, revealing a bright burst of light.

Passing inside, they entered a brightly lit roomed, filled with ornate and intricately carved wooden furniture, mainly low chairs with big soft cushions on top that were themselves brightly coloured and richly embroidered.

'Sit' said Annie, and she and Yvonna went through another door, leaving Erin and Francesca alone. Erin sat on a small chair that had a carved lion standing proudly across the back, with a black cushion embroidered with a golden bird of some sort. Francesca sat opposite her, taking off her hat.

Erin could see that she was indeed a large lady, but built in a very motherly way, with sparkling blue eyes, and a kind face like the other two sisters. Feeling bold, Erin asked:

'Are you all real sisters?'

Francesca smiled.

'Not by birth' she said, 'but certainly sisters in adversity I suppose. But let's wait and eat before the questions.'

As if in confirmation of this, Erin's stomach rumbled and Francesca smiled again. With superb timing, the other two sisters appeared carrying food, along with drink. Francesca pulled over a low table and with a clatter of china and the meal was laid out on top.

It was a bit of an odd looking meal, thought Erin. The drinks looked normal, just glasses of lemonade, but on a large plate in the middle of the table was a huge round biscuit, the biggest Erin had ever seen.

'Shortbread' said Yvonna in explanation, 'although maybe it should be called Largebread' she smiled, and Erin giggled.
The meal was nice; she had a large chunk of shortbread on a plate and a glass of lemonade. Not a green vegetable in sight.
'Perfect!' thought Erin.

But the meal was soon over and the ladies fussed over the tidying up, clearing everything away. Then they all returned and sat in chairs with Erin, so they were all in a circle.
'Are you tired?' asked Annie.
Erin wasn't tired; she had slept while Handy took her on her long trip up the mountains.
Francesca then said:
'It's time to tell you a few things then Erin, so please pay attention.' And she began.

Francesca started off by saying that the hard part of understanding all this was that it was just so hard to understand. Erin didn't think that was very helpful. However, as Francesca continued to explain, with some help from the sisters, it started to make some sense.

Apparently, most children believe that their toys come alive at night and live some kind of double life. Erin had been told that by Stephane, so she was OK there, but this double life happened in a slightly different world, which was why people rarely saw it. So when Erin saw a toy car, it was just a toy car, but in another world it was driving around and being a toy car *at the same time.*

That was why, they explained, that in Erin's world, time would be passing and people coming and going, but in her world, toys and indeed many other things were inanimate objects, but in this world, they were, basically, alive.

Francesca then asked: 'Tell me, do you feel different to the way you normally feel?'

The sister had put her finger on something that had been nagging at Erin ever since this started. She had indeed felt different, somehow older, more grown up in some way, aware that she was thinking 'older' thoughts as it were.

She pondered this with a frown and Francesca smiled. 'I see you have' she said, 'for in this place, what exists is not just the object or the person but the idea of what makes up that object or person. So you see, you are Erin, not just as you are now, but as you will be. Otherwise, how would you understand all this? How have you managed to run away from spiders and ride on a sock monster? Little Erin would never have done this.' Then she added with a smile, 'At least not straight away.'

This was a lot to take in, but there was an obvious question that Erin needed to ask.

'So why am I here?' The sisters all glanced at each other and it was Annie who spoke up after some hesitation.

'There is an evil force in this world. Of course, evil and good have always lived together. But something very bad has grown here and is infecting everything around it. Now, ordinarily, that evil can't affect your world. But this evil can.'

'How?' asked Erin.

'Spiders' replied Yvonna.

Yvonna then added:

'In your world, in ancient times, when people wanted to do magic such as heal someone who was very ill, they would take a poison, not a poison to kill themselves, but one which would take them to another world, a place where they could confront the evil spirits and defeat them and so cure their patients. Theoretically, large amounts of spider venom can move people between one world and the next in the same way. But a while ago, a huge and powerful spider arrived here from your world, and has a venom so concentrated that just a small amount can move you from your world to this. That's how you got here.'

Erin pondered this and added thoughtfully:

'I felt a small sting on my finger, just before everything changed.' The sisters looked at each other again, nodding as if they had just heard something they knew.

Now all children treat their bedroom as a sort of gigantic rubbish bin. Every now and again, at the prompting of parents, children have to tidy their room. Kids don't know why, after all, they know where everything is. This rule also works for husbands, who know where everything is in the shed, even though it looks a mess, and when their wife tidies it for them they complain bitterly that they just can't find anything anymore.

At some time in the past, a few years earlier, Auntie Lizzie had bought a sandwich. Nobody knew what type of sandwich it was. But she had hidden the sandwich in its plastic wrapper under her mattress, and then forgotten about it.
So it had gone mouldy.
Green mouldy, then white mouldy, then black slimy.
Still it stayed there, and had gone slimier, and darker, until it became a black slimy, syrupy mass. Who knows what revolting smell would have been released had the packet burst.

But at that point, a curious spider had investigated. It was only a small house spider, investigating the world. It had clambered onto the packet from below in between the springs. Now it was curiously poking the plastic wrapper, and the questioning spiked tip of its leg had pierced the bulging surface.

It is hard to say what happened at this point, but there was tidal surge of black within the packet and somehow it been sucked inside, never to be seen again.

But in that instant the poison in the sandwich, plus the spider's own venom had unexpectedly opened a door into the world of the Dolly Sisters, but what had come through the door was a dull, black, hairy, enormous, menacing spider. He wasn't as dark as night, he almost *was* night.

Francesca whispered 'He is much more than just a black spider, he seems to radiate darkness, and at times he is surrounded by a small moving cloud that is as dark and cold as the blackness of space.'

He had almost immediately been able to bring the spiders under control, and was gradually taking over the rest of the room. But his ultimate cunning plan was to use the venom that he now carried in his poison sacs, in order to bring a human into their world.

And, the sisters told Erin, he wanted that human because if he could capture one, with the help of the special venom, he could invade their mind, and return to the other world, living in the head of his victim, living their life and doing whatever he liked. But more importantly, he could start making more venom, and slowly bring all of Erin's world under control as well as this one.

So now Erin understood. The sting wasn't just to bring her here, it was to capture her and use her as a way of getting back. And then, what would he do?

She thought of her brother and her mum. She thought of all her family and friends and wondered what an evil mind could do to them or anyone else. Now she didn't laugh. In fact, she felt a cold knot of dread in her stomach; it was as if a kind of dark fate was stalking her.

Now who would have thought an evil sandwich could cause such trouble? Children, tidy your rooms, you never know what evil you are letting loose upon the world!

‘Things are actually worse than that’ explained Francesca. Erin was pretty much wide awake now, if rather shocked, so she just nodded quietly at this point.

Francesca went on: ‘We can’t actually stop this from happening you know, we just don’t have the numbers or the power to do it. But you do.’

‘Me!’ asked Erin. ‘Why me?’

‘We found this spider quite soon after he arrived and was gathering more spiders to join him.’ said Francesca. ‘We had sent out a patrol of fairies, who caught him out in the open as he crossed the floor. They dived down and several of their spears pierced his body. But he just sat there, hissing at us. It seems that anyone from this world cannot kill him. We have consulted together, and asked a very wise friend and have found that because he originally came from your world, I’m afraid only you, or someone like you can actually kill him.’

Now it’s all very well telling someone that they are becoming the idea of what they will be, and that you aren't quite the vulnerable little girl that you are in the real world.

And it's all very well that a young girl has just had some amazing adventures and may be feeling much stronger and more confident than she used to be.

Because inside Erin, this new, more grown up and stronger idea of Erin had just met the headlong wall of terror of a little girl who was stuck in an awful place and was just about to be overwhelmed by an enormous wave of fear. Erin suddenly leapt up, dashing under the arms of the surprised ladies, she headed for the door, but she couldn't see any way of opening it.

'Stop her sisters!' exclaimed Francesca, but in a soft voice, she didn't want to frighten the girl. Erin gave up looking for the door handle and ran back into the room, the ladies fussed and flustered after her, but she was small and fast and dodged around them and under them.

Dashing over to the other side of the room, she shot behind a long, low sofa, intending to dash back to the door. As she put her hand on the wall to steady herself, she seemed to touch a carving that moved under her hand, and before she could do anything about it, a panel in the floor opened and she slid down a short, smooth ramp into a dark space.

The panel had closed behind her, she had no idea where she was, and she was tired, so she lay there, panting slightly, her head whirling with all the things that had happened to her.

It was such a jumble of images that kept leaping at her, the bouncing clown, the nasty spiders, a huge glass penguin, a sock monster called Handy, three dolls who were sisters... well, sometimes nature takes its course and this time she did cry as she lay there helpless, crying silently in the dark, big wet tears rolling down her face.

But Erin is becoming a strong girl, and her tears stopped and she took a deep breath. Inside her there was always a little hard shell of determination, previously very useful in getting her own way at home. That determination had just met the Idea of Erin and they decided to get together and sort things out. She took a deep breath, and sat up.

Everything was totally black, and she did manage a grimace followed by a weak smile. As if in response to her smile, a soft light sprang up ahead of her, and she could see that she was in a room with shiny black walls, black ceiling and black floor. For a second she thought she had wandered into Auntie Claire's teenage bedroom.

The soft light was coming from a glass ball that seemed to hang in the air in front of her, and as she walked towards it, it rose slowly up in the air above her head and attached itself to the ceiling.

The light revealed a hooded figure, sitting on the floor with head bowed. Erin stood still for a second or two, then carefully walked towards the figure that was either asleep or in deep thought.
She stopped suddenly as the figure raised its head and pulled the hood back. Staring calmly and

intently at her was a man of indeterminate age, with a bald head, and piercing blue almond shaped eyes that shone slightly in the dim light.

Erin didn't know anything about Japan, if she had, she would have thought 'Japanese.'

'Welcome young Erin', he said in a melodious soft voice, and he gestured with his arm for her to sit. 'Welcome to my house' he said.

'Your house?'

'Oh yes, it is my Japanese lacquer box house.' he answered. 'I share it with the sisters, but I live in this quiet and secret place most of the time.'

'It's dark' Erin commented. 'Everything is dark.'

The man smiled and made a sign in the air with his hand, and the light grew a little brighter. Black seemed to be the colour of choice, even the man was wearing a black robe, with a black silk belt.

'You can call me Po Kang,' he said.

Erin giggled, it sounded a little like 'poking.' Po Kang smiled again. 'Your sense of humour will keep you strong' he stated, 'as well as your inner strength' Erin sighed.

'Everyone seems to expect so much of me.' she said softly. 'It's not my fault I am here, I want to go home.'

'You will go home' promised Po Kang, 'but I'm afraid it can only be at the right time.'
She sighed deeply again.

'I have something for you' said Po Kang. Reaching behind him he picked up a long, thin, black case of some kind of darkly polished wood.

Opening it, he very carefully removed a long, samurai sword. Resting the blade on the palms of his hands, he held it out to her. She looked at it, and wondered what on earth she wanted a shiny sharp stick for.
He looked up. 'Take it' he commanded, 'it has been waiting for you.'

'But...' she started to protest, then found her gaze locked in his as he added in a quiet but forcible voice:

'You must take it; it has been waiting for you.' She reached out a nervous hand.

'Be careful' he advised, 'The blade is very sharp. Use the handle.'

Grasping the handle, she held the sword up to the light. It was amazingly light, and the blade wasn't just shiny, it seemed to have waves of colour that danced under its metallic sheen. She turned it slightly one way then another, marvelling at the way the colours moved, almost as if they were alive under the surface.

'It's very beautiful' she whispered.

Po Kang smiled. 'It is an ancient weapon, made with skill and deep knowledge of metalwork and what I suppose you would call magic.'

Erin knew what was coming next.

'It's for me to stick in the slimy sandwich spider, isn't it?' she asked with some bitterness.

Po Kang paused a little before solemnly affirming:

'Yes it is.'

'Oh well, I might as well get on with it.' she said with resignation and started to get up. Po Kang smiled again.

'Please, sit little one' he said, and added 'there are some things we must do first.' As she

squatted back down, he handed her a scabbard and belt.
'You need to keep the sword in here' he explained, 'you can't run around waving a sword, you'll hurt yourself.'
Erin carefully slid the bright blade into the scabbard and slung the belt over her shoulder.

Po Kang then told her there was one last thing he had to do. He asked her to bow her head, and she jumped a little as she felt his hands softly touch her hair. As he did so, he muttered soft, foreign sounding words under his breath, and she felt a sort of golden feeling of calmness gradually roll through her.

It reminded her of warm summer mornings, or that lovely feeling you have in the morning after a long nights sleep and you lie in bed all warm and toasty, wrapped in sheets and duvet, and totally relaxed. She remembered that back at school there had been a visitor in the school assembly who had taught the children how to relax by slowing down their breathing and imagining a lovely place in their mind where they would feel safe, and that they could go to this safe place in their mind any time they felt sad or angry.

The feeling was a bit like that, but something else seemed to be happening too, because mixed in with all that golden loveliness was a sort of not unpleasant tingle, and she almost felt as if she was changing somehow.

As she looked down at herself and almost felt as if everything about her was slightly bigger.

'Growing' she whispered to herself. Indeed in a totally impossible way to explain she was starting to understand the world slightly differently, as if she was a little taller, or older. She could almost feel herself growing from the inside out. Not by much, just a little, but certainly something had changed.

'Stand up' Po Kang ordered, and she did. 'How do you feel?' he asked her.

'Taller' she replied, and added, 'What have you done to me?'

'I found the Idea of Erin in your mind, the potential of everything that you are, and everything that you either will be or can be' he replied, 'and I gave her some of my power. You will feel stronger now.'

Something in the tone of his voice had changed, and as she looked down at Po Kang, she noticed that he looked a bit older, even slightly transparent; she felt she could almost see the walls and floor through him. Sensing her observation, he looked at her with his older eyes and reassured her.

'It is OK, I have given you some of my strength and wisdom, I will fade now, but I am always here. Be brave and strong Erin and you will be home soon.'

Even as he was speaking, he was fading, almost blending into the darkness. As he vanished, a door in the wall slid open and Erin stepped through. She was back outside the lacquer box house. Waiting for her outside were the sisters, who were smiling broadly at her.

'You have met Po Kang' said Yvonna

'And now you are our little hero' added Annie, and to Erin's astonishment, they all bowed low.

Annie and Yvonna then came forward and each kissed Erin on the cheek, before hugging her and going back into the house. Francesca remained, and she put her hands on Erin's shoulders and gave her the final instructions.

'Handy will be waiting for you where he left you, ride him to the bottom of the mountains, where he will leave you. There will be more friends waiting there, who will lead you across the Used Tissue swamp. Once across the swamp, they will attack the spiders to keep them busy, so that you can head straight under the bed for the far corner. There you will find the black spider, and the door.'

Erin nodded. Francesca went on: 'Use the sword on the spider, it can cut anything, so even if you get caught and tied up with spider web, you can cut through it easily. His power cannot match you or the sword. Once he is dead, run like mad for the corner, because the door will close soon after.'
Erin noticed there was a tear in Francesca's eye.
'It will be dangerous Erin, but you are bigger and stronger now, and I know you can do this.
Remember that you are not just a little girl now. Po Kang has helped you become everything you ever

will be and can be. There is nothing stronger than that.'

There didn't seem much that Erin could say, so she hugged Francesca tightly and turned quickly away. As she vanished into the gloom, Francesca turned away sadly.

Erin soon got back to the giant glass penguin. Wrapping the rope around her, the penguin lowered her back down to the mountain top, where she undid the rope and the penguin hauled it back up. With a very deep sigh, she shifted the sword belt a little and turned around to find Handy.

Meanwhile, just as Erin was looking for Handy, in the deep dark under the bed, a large group of spiders were assembled, and they all seemed to be staring at one spot in front of them-a large, inky cloud of black.

The spiders were quivering with excitement, anticipation, and perhaps even fear.

The cloud swirled and started to become more solid, the swirls gradually merging into the shape of a huge monstrous spider, much bigger than all the others, with multiple red eyes, a fat bloated body and murderous sting that was so heavy it dragged along the floor.

As the huge spider became solid, the other smaller spiders crouched down low in supplication, and listened avidly as the monster started to speak.

The light was fairly dim, but Erin could still see the shape of the bedroom and the huge bed looming to the right. But Handy was nowhere to be seen. She didn't want to risk shouting out loud, so she just tried to shout softly. Her calls for Handy seemed to go unanswered, and there was no movement around her. So she decided to wait a little.

Crouching down low, she listened intently for any sound of him. But being alone on a mountain top in a strange and hostile place is not pleasant, and every faint noise seemed to have evil intent. She decided that it seemed evident that Handy was not going to turn up. Nothing for it but to trek down the mountain on her own.

Now we have previously mentioned that a mountain range made of dirty clothing is not easy to negotiate, but has a much softer fall should you slip. Erin did start out quite gingerly at first, picking her way carefully down, holding on tightly where she could and placing her feet with care. But it was a long way down and after a while the bottom seemed no nearer.

'Bother this!' she thought to herself as she gazed from the small ledge she was on that looked like a sleeve, and examined what may have been part of a woolly jumper a few feet below. Taking care not to miss, she aimed for a part of the jumper below that looked safe and jumped. For a few scary seconds she fell then landed and bounced on the soft material.

'That's the way to do it!' she whispered in triumph, and that indeed was what she did, walking where it was easy, but jumping when she could, in fact she started to enjoy it, and was even giggling quietly as she fell through the air and bounced up and down on landing.

Not usually the way to climb down a mountain boys and girls, so please don't try this at home.

Very quickly, she seemed to reach the foothills and was much closer to the floor. Ahead of her in the middle distance was the white expanse of the marshes, to her right, the flat plain of the floor. At was at this point that something happened.

Poised for another jump, she was aiming at what looked like a trouser leg below her. She jumped, laughing, but when she hit the trouser leg, the material seemed to tip to one side, and suddenly she was tumbling down a dark crevasse, over and over, banging against the soft sides, but falling, falling. Until she finally landed on her back on something soft, but looking up, all she could see was the deep ravine towering over her.

Imagine being trapped in a giant laundry basket, for that's what it was like. Think of that stale, dirty clothes smell, and then try to imagine how hard it would be to actually climb out of if you were only a few inches high. The very softness and suppleness of the clothes that had allowed her to bounce her way down the mountain, were now stopping her from climbing back up. Every time she tried, she just succeeded in pulling some fabric down. Try as she might, she just couldn't get anywhere, and indeed she had to stop because her efforts just seemed to be pulling more and more fabric down and she realised that she might actually end up not being able to get out at all.

‘I need to think’ she said to herself.
So she sat down and stared upwards, trying to figure out a way to get out, but it just seemed hopeless. Her eyes by now had got used to the darkness, so she could dimly see what was around her. As she looked around, she noticed that the cloth around her was in folds, not too surprising, but the folds of course were big, and looked almost like soft tunnels. So she started to wonder if she could burrow her way to safety.

‘It might work’, she thought, ‘But what if I can’t breathe? What if the clothes collapse around me and I can’t move?’ Well, she certainly couldn’t stay where she was. So she looked for a wide enough fold that looked as if it would head in the right direction for her, and pushed her way in.
If she had known what claustrophobia was, she felt it now, for as she pushed in, the folds seemed to close behind her, so although she could move forward, it looked as if she may have trouble turning around. It was dusty and smelly, little bits of fluff started to get up her nose and she snuffled, trying hard not to sneeze. The most awful thought was that the tunnel would come to a dead end, and

maybe all she was doing was burrowing into a pocket, and would have to fight her way back if she could find it. Maybe she would be stuck burrowing in here until she lost her strength and gave up, gasping in a soft smelly coffin, slowly suffocating. In a way, this was more frightening than anything she had ever done before.

But she carried on. She was getting hot and sweaty too, pushing and crawling her way in what she hoped was the right direction. She was given hope by the fact that the fabric seemed to change, so she was moving from one type of garment to another, which suggested she was in between garments rather than stuck inside one. Soon, the fabric turned to white cotton, like a shirt, and it was much easier to push to one side, and not as heavy. While she was in the shirt, she decided to have a rest, so she pushed the material out into a small hole so that it wasn't so claustrophobic. The sword on her back hadn't helped, it stuck out and would catch every now and then on the fabric, so she had to tug a bit harder.

At this point, something occurred to her that may have occurred to all of you readers out there. She pulled the scabbard round and slid the sword out. 'Hmmm' she thought, 'a sharp object will cut fabric. I am so dim!'

Being very careful with the blade, she poked it upwards and slid it across. It pierced the white linen easily, and she pushed her head through. There was more white around her, so, standing up, she shoved the sword out in front of her, and rather like a jungle explorer, she slashed the sword from side to side and made her way forwards.

It wasn't quite as simple as it seemed, the fabric still closed around her, but she was at least able to stand and move forwards, so with one hand slashing and the other holding the fabric up away from her head, she carried on. Very soon she saw that she was standing on carpet instead of linen, so she reasoned she must be close to the edge of the mountain. Slowing down and cutting much more carefully, she pushed forwards, until one of her slashes revealed open air, and she was through.

Moving much more carefully now, with a few silent cuts, she made a hole big enough to go through. Poking her head out slowly, she looked out. The floor stretched away in front of her, looking to her left, she saw the jumble of the mountain where it reached the floor, and in the distance, a hint of white showed where the swamp began. It was a little way away, but she had come out fairly close. Looking all around, she could see nothing, so she carefully emerged, thankful to be in the fresh air again.

Thinking it was best to keep the sword in hand and crouching slightly, she moved carefully towards the swamp, hugging the mountains to her left and trying not to make a sound. Creeping slowly on, the swamp drew closer and she could make out the whiteness of it, and the fact that it looked sort of lumpy, like a pile of low lying clouds rather than a swamp. Just in front of her, the mountains came to an end, with a long sleeve trailing onto the floor. As she approached the sleeve, it seemed to bulge in places, and she could see it moving as something began to emerge from the end of the sleeve.

'Handy!' she thought with relief, but then she froze completely still as a huge spider emerged, and stood there, silently sniffing the air.

Heart stopping moment?
Very nearly!

Heart in her mouth, she stayed as still as she could. Her breathing sounded loud in her ears, and suddenly her palms were sweaty and the hand holding the sword started to shake a little. There was a feeling of something booming in her chest and her ears and she realised it was her heart thumping like a giant bass drum.

The spider had stopped dead still and was moving its head ever so slightly from side to side as if trying to scent something. This spider was at least twice the size of the ones she had seen earlier, and had a much bigger black body, with a splash of red colour on the back like clotted blood.

She could only think of freezing in place and hope the spider go away. And indeed that is what it seemed to do, it turned away as if to go back where it had come from, when suddenly its head whipped round and stared straight at her. Before she had a chance to do anything at all, it leapt high in the air with astonishing speed, trailing a strand of web behind it. As Erin twisted to face it, raising her sword slightly, it landed behind her, leapt again, and the strand of web whipped itself around her, trapping her sword arm against her body. With her free hand, she tugged desperately at the web, but as soon as she touched it, that hand was caught as well. She was desperate now and frantically tried to pull herself free, but it was far too late, the spider dashed around and around her, and in a few seconds, she was wrapped up tight. She opened her mouth to shout for help, but with a final swift whip of web, a strand wrapped itself around her face, covering her mouth, and she was then wrapped from head to toe by the web, the spider leaving only her nose and eyes uncovered. Unable to do anything to steady herself, she fell to the ground in her cocoon of spider silk. Although she could breathe through her nose, the strand covering her mouth tasted bitter and sticky, and she felt like she was suffocating. As she lay there helpless, the spider stalked towards her.

'Yesssssss' it hissed. 'I have caught you little girl, my lord will be sssso pleasssed.' Erin struggled futilely, and mumbled something behind her gag. The spider seemed to laugh a soft hissing laugh. It bent its head towards her, and she screamed under her gag as the horrible head drew closer. It seemed to have several eyes, all one colour, and large, horrible fangs that were opening and closing with an obscene insect clicking noise. It was enjoying her panic and hissed with laughter again.

'Maybe I could keep you to myself, yessssss' it hissed, 'take you home, hang you up in my larder and wait for you to go all soft and soggy, yessssss.' It hissed with hideous laughter again.
'Or maybe I can bite your sweet head off and sssssuck all your squishy insides out.'
Erin thought she would die with fear, being so helpless and she continued to scream under her awful gag, much to the continued amusement of the spider that hissed in horrible imitation of her every time she made a sound.

Trying to control herself and beat back the waves of panic, she forced herself to stop screaming, determined not to let the spider continue to mock her. Then, with a flick of its legs, it threw her onto its back, whipped a few strands around her to hold her tight, and scuttled off across the floor.

This was a horrible nightmare for her; the spider's fast and almost silent scuttling was unnatural and seemed to frighten her at some deep primeval level. She could feel the harsh hairs on its back rub against her as it ran, it had a rank smell, and the web across her mouth was tasting more and more foul.

She was in despair now, the spider was so big and fast, she just could not see a way to escape. She thought with despair that she would soon reach the big evil spider from her world, and that would be the end of everything. Or maybe just be taken away somewhere dark and dismal to hang in the air and provide torment and fun for this evil creature. She still had her sword, but it was securely wrapped against her body with no way she could use it.

What she did notice though, was that the spider was not going in the direction she expected it to. Instead of heading for the gaping dark under the bed, it was heading in the opposite direction, straight for the bookcase.

'Maybe it has a lair under the bookcase' she thought to herself. This did give her a little hope, although the situation was still desperate. The spider was fast though, and it seemed to cross the floor very quickly.

Suddenly, she started to rise in the air, and she realised that the spider was climbing up the bookcase rather than running underneath it. It could climb as fast as it could run, and as they went up at a fast pace, she watched with a stomach churning vertigo as the floor quickly slipped from sight. She could still see the white swamps and the mountains, with the huge bed in the vague distance. The bookcase was higher up than the cupboard she had visited earlier, and she fancied that she could almost make out the black Japanese box and the giant penguin away in the distance. But there was nothing between her and a dizzying drop to her death, so she closed her eyes as she felt nausea churn at the back of her throat and decided to wait until they had stopped.

The upward motion came to a halt eventually, and the spider continued forwards, this time slower.

She couldn't see anything around her now, but knew that once the spider stopped, it may be her only chance. Provided of course that it decided to unwrap her. She tried very hard to conquer her fear, and steeled herself to take advantage of any opportunity that she may seize.

The spider did indeed stop, and with a flick of a couple of its legs, it cut the webs holding her to its back, and dropped her on the floor. Not much she could do yet as she was still securely wrapped, but she had landed on her back, and what she could see now was a giant lamp that towered over her, obviously a desk lamp, but not lit. Standing over her, the spider picked her up with one leg and scuttled up the lamp, and with a swift flung strand of web and quick twist of its legs, she was hanging suspended in her cocoon, dangling from the light.

Hanging beside her, it moved her so that it could look into her eyes. 'Yessss, you will hang here my sweet tasty treat, and when you are runny, you will be my dinner, yesssss. And once I have supped, I will take the sword to my lord, and your pretty head, and he will give me pressssents, yesssssss.'

And with that it scuttled away, and left her in the dark, swinging from the lamp, alone and very scared.
She was so far up, she could see very little. She tried struggling against her bonds, but they were stuck fast, and the movement only made her swing violently, so that she bashed herself against the pillar of the lamp. Her hand still holding the sword was also bound tightly and she just couldn't move it at all. If she had despaired earlier, that feeling was nothing compared to how she felt now, and she felt stinging tears of anger and fear well up in her eyes.

But she could hear a few sounds though. Sometimes there was the clicking, pattering sound of the spider as it scuttled below, maybe hunting for more food. She could also faintly hear other sounds that were just too distant to make out. So she swung there, like a broken yoyo, alone in the dark.

All too soon she thought she heard the spider come back, she felt the vibration of it as it climbed up the lamp. Then something turned her around, and she expected to see the champing jaws and glittering eyes of the spider, but to her complete astonishment, instead she was looking into the unblinking eyes of what could only be described as a giant lizard.

She was way beyond screaming now, so she stared back, frozen, not sure if she was in a worse predicament than before. A thin tongue flickered out of the lizards' mouth and swiftly ran over her face, and as if satisfied with what it had found, the lizard turned and scuttled away back down the lamp post.

'Weird' she thought. Especially as nothing much happened, so she assumed it was a passing curious creature having a look and wondering what was going on. So she swung silently in the dark, formless plans of escape running headlong through her mind, all of them useless and having only one end.

Then came a sound she hadn't heard before, a fluttering noise that seemed familiar.

'Bird?' she thought and realised that the sound was somehow faster and more high pitched than a bird. At all events it was getting closer and as it did so, she thought she recognised it, having heard it before last year on a wonderful summer holiday, back in her other life.

'Dragonfly?' she whispered. It was a fast hum, the sort that is made by large insect wings. That was unsettling too, as she started to wonder if there were giant wasps or bees in here as well.

She wriggled in her bonds, and managed to swing around slowly so she could at least see what was coming. Peering into the gloom, she spotted a distant shape moving through the air below her, heading her way. There was a fast moving fuzziness at the back of the figure that suggested wings rapidly moving, and it was indeed rapid, for it rose quickly, shooting towards her until it stopped, right in front of her.

'Oh wow' Erin whispered in awe. For the creature wasn't a creature at all, but an incredibly beautiful lady, hovering there like a human humming bird. Her eyes were shining a bright fluorescent blue in the dim light, and she seemed to be dressed from neck to feet in a tight fitting green garment that looked as if it was made of small feathers, or scales. At any event, it shimmered and reflected what little light there was.

The creature, or maybe fairy, reached out two hands and cupped Erin's' face in her hands.

'Poor little one' she murmured. 'Don't worry; I will have you out of here in a trice.'
The fairy flew up, although Erin couldn't see what she was doing, she felt herself being lowered gently to the ground. The fairy then stooped over her and produced a knife that shimmered as if made of black glass, and swiftly sawed through Erin's web bonds. Erin sighed with relief as the fairy gently removed the strand from round her mouth.

'Thank you' gasped Erin as she opened her mouth wide and breathed in deeply.
'My pleasure my Lady' replied the fairy with a smile, and she continued pulling away at the strands sticking to Erin until they were all off and lying in a pile on the floor. Erin put the sword down and rubbed at her sore skin gently, the sticky spider stands had left it feeling sore and stinging.

But just then, Erin heard a fast pattering of feet and a voice loudly hissing 'Thievesssssssssssss' and the giant spider leaped over her head, landing full on the fairy.

The fairy twisted in the spiders grip, putting both her hands under its head, trying to hold off the crashing jaws. The fairy was twisting and writhing as well, for at the back of the spiders bloated belly was a large sting that the spider was stabbing with. The pair rolled over and over, the spider hissing and stabbing, and the fairy grunting and gasping with the effort of holding back the spiders head and avoiding the thrusting poison spike.

Erin's heart was hammering in her chest as she watched this terrible fight. She bent down and grabbed her sword, running over to where the spider and fairy were locked in a death battle. She raised the sword in the air, but she had to hesitate. Not only had she never killed anything before, but she was afraid of missing, or hitting her rescuer.

The fairy shot her a glance as she rolled, locked in the deadly embrace of the spider.

'Kill it!' she shouted, 'you can do it!'

Taking a deep breath, Erin raised the sword over her head and plunged it down. Unfortunately, she not only missed, she had thrust it into the wooden bookcase top, and now the sword was stuck fast, with Erin frantically pulling at it. The fairy was tiring, and Erin could see the spiders' jaws getting closer to the fairy's face despite its desperate attempts to hold it back. The fairy looked past Erin and suddenly shouted loudly,
'Close your eyes Erin, NOW!'

She did so, and flinched as a blinding white light exploded even through her closed eyes. Opening her eyes just a little, despite the glaring harshness of the light she saw that the fairy was now lying panting on the ground, while the spider writhed and hissed upside down nearby, in obvious pain.

'The light......... the light.........' it hissed, 'it burnsssss'. Without thinking, Erin grasped her sword handle and heaved it free, then with a determination that surprised her; she walked over to the spider, and with hardly a second thought thrust the sword home in the spider's belly.

To her horror it hissed and writhed, jaws champing and foam spitting from its mouth. Its convulsions pulled the sword from her grasp and for a horrible moment she imagined the spider rolling over and getting back to its feet, but there was black blood now bubbling around the ghastly wound, and it twitched and lay still.

'Well done child' the fairy praised her, as she rose to her feet. Erin turned and saw the giant lizard standing by the large button at the base of the desk lamp. 'Spiders hate the light,' the fairly explained, 'it hurts them. You did a brave thing, well done.'
Erin hung her head and whispered:
'I've never killed anything before.'
The fairy put a reassuring arm around her shoulder.
'You did well' she told her softly. 'But we must hurry now'. The fairy walked over to the dead spider and pulled the sword free, handing it to Erin, who slid it into its scabbard. The fairy then gestured to the lizard and it pressed the light switch down. Darkness suddenly descended, except for the bright after image of the light that hung in the air in front of her, slowly fading.

'Don't worry' said a voice in her ear 'I can see in the dark. Here, take my hand.'

Erin felt the thin but strong hand of the fairy take hers and they started to walk quickly across the top of the bookcase. Somewhere behind her she could hear the heavy patter of the lizard as it followed.

'The spiders will have seen the light' the soft voice said, 'and now they will be looking for us. But, I have a place to hide.'

'Who are you?' asked Erin. The fairy lady laughed softly.

'Pardon my manners' she responded. 'My name is Anyiko, I am a Bookcase Fairy. Bookcase of course because that is where I live.'

'You know my name?' Erin replied.

'Yes I do. And I know your quest. But we must hurry now. Can you see?'

Erin nodded, and the fairy took her in her arms, effortlessly and they rose in the air, fairy wings whirring, before suddenly swooping downwards past the top of the bookcase and then inwards before landing.

‘We are just under the top shelf’ whispered Anyiko as she let go of Erin but kept hold of her hand. Erin could see a long stack of giant books away to the left, in front of her was a huge square box, bigger than the Japanese box of the Dolly Sisters, and it looked much more solid. It was at least as big as a large house; the outside was obviously wooden, with a dark grain running across it.

The box was raised up on strong feet, so all she could see was a dark space underneath, about a foot high, and that was where they were heading. The gap underneath was small, and tight. Anyiko dropped to her stomach and started to crawl underneath, gesturing for Erin to follow. Erin dropped to her knees and followed the fairy. The gap was very tight indeed, as she had to lie on her stomach, and her head was just touching the bottom of the box above her. She had to stop and slip off the sword belt and hold it as she crawled. Dust was getting into her eyes and throat and she sneezed, banging her head hard on the wood above her. Distracted, she didn’t notice that the fairy had stopped so she banged into her feet.

'Ow!' she complained loudly. The fairy in front of her shooshed her into silence, and added,

'We're there now' and disappeared from view upwards. Erin crawled over to where Anyiko had been, and a slim hand appeared from above grabbed her arm and lifted her upwards.

She found herself lifted into a large space, obviously the inside of the box. The fairy dropped a thick wooden hatch into place where they had crawled through and pulled a woollen rug across the top.

Erin gazed around her; the inside of the box was painted a bright red, with the grain of the wood showing through. She thought that it was as big as her school hall, the wooden floor reminding her of school and a life that seemed very remote right at this moment.

There was plenty of light inside from several candles set around the walls, and it wasn't furnished as such, although there seemed to be a lot of empty boxes scattered around the room, as well as some large cushions and blankets that had been piled into a corner. There also seemed to be some heaps of what looked like weapons; mainly spears and swords.

So much for the box, but what Erin really noticed were the people, or perhaps it would be more accurate to say -the occupants. She could see winged fairies like Anyiko, a couple of bouncing clowns, some dolls, and several short, rather hairy troll-like creatures.

When Erin and Anyiko had entered, all of them stopped whatever they were doing and crowded around them, uttering calls of welcome.
Anyiko held up her hands and everyone fell silent. 'Time for meetings later' she declared. 'There is a spider hunt on'

At this, everyone suddenly became busy, grabbing weapons and blankets, and taking up what looked like well rehearsed positions, some standing by the hatch, others around the walls or in the centre, and all facing inwards, although they seemed to be looking nervously down at the floor.

Anyiko took Erin by the hand, grabbed a couple of blankets and led her to a corner. When they got there, all the candles in the room were extinguished and the room became inky black and silent.

'You must sit down and be very quiet now' whispered Anyiko. Erin squeezed her hand to let her know that she understood and sat down. The silence and the darkness wrapped them round like an inky blanket, and Erin fancied that her carefully quiet breath was loud and rasping in the silence. Somehow a room full of people trying their best to keep quiet makes even the tiniest sound boom like an explosion, but everyone else seemed accustomed to this situation and silence did indeed reign.

It wasn't long before Erin heard a distant pattering of feet that she recognised as a spiders, but there was more than one spider making the noise, there must have been dozens of them, and she realised that they were running all over the box, on the sides, on the top and underneath. She even fancied she could hear their hissing breath as they searched. The tension was intolerable as everyone hiding knew that the slightest sound could give their position away.

Eventually though the noise of the spiders feet faded, but still everyone remained silent. Anyiko bent down and whispered very carefully in her ear, 'No sound until you hear the signal' and squeezed Erin's' hand in reassurance.

Whenever you need to be quiet, you can be sure that you feel the urge to sneeze, or cough, and Erin felt a dryness in her throat that was becoming more and more irritating as she waited. She tried swallowing to wet the dry spot at the back of her throat, but it made no difference, and the overwhelming urge to cough just grew and grew.

Just as she thought she could stand it no longer, there came a rapid series of knocks on the outside of the box, which made her jump in fright.
'It's OK, it's the signal' said Anyiko. 'We are safe now.'

All around them they heard people stirring and moving about, and light came back into the room as candles and lamps were lit. The same knocking came on the floor where the trapdoor was. Anyiko twitched the rug covering the trapdoor to one side and lifted it up.

A lizard head with twitching tongue poked itself up through the hole. Anyiko reached into a pocket and produced what looked like a small piece of cooked meat which the lizard whisked off her hand with its tongue, and then swiftly turned and vanished back into the gloom.

Now that they were safe and the room was lit again, all the people gathered around Erin and Anyiko and began to talk about what to do next.

The general impression that Erin had was that this was a group of some kind of rebels or freedom fighters. There was a lot of loud and angry shouting about the spiders and especially a name she kept hearing over and over again - Kurtees.

'Who is Kurtees?' she asked Anyiko while the group chattered and complained.

'Kurtees is the worst evil we have seen in this world for a long time.' replied the fairy. 'I know that you have been told of him already. His spider body is shrouded in darkness, so that it is hard to see him; his shape is indistinct, as if he is enclosed in an evil black smoke. We think that he is so hard to see not only because of the evil that is in him, but also because he exists in both your world and this'

Being reminded of the nasty spider didn't cheer up Erin one tiny bit, but then someone tapped her on the shoulder and she looked up into the brightly coloured face of a clown. The clown wasn't smiling under the paint though.

'Pardon me' said the clown, 'I wonder if you have seen my friend Stephane?'

'I am sorry' replied Erin, 'Last time I saw him he was being taken away by some spiders.'

The clown hung his head and she saw a tear streak its way down his white make-up.

'I thought it might be so.' he whispered slowly, and hung his head and turned away. Erin plucked his sleeve and added reassuringly

'I am sorry, he was very nice.' The clown looked back and nodded,

'He was indeed.'

Erin felt sorry for him so she added,

'But I am here to help kill the spider'.

The clown shook his head and looked down at her, saying

'You are only a little girl, I don't think so' and wandered away.

Erin felt hugely sad at this, and watched as the clown wandered over to where the other clowns were standing and she could see them talking, looking over at her and shaking their heads as if in doubt.

Meanwhile, the debate amongst the others had seemed to end and Anyiko turned to her, with the others standing silently behind her.

'We are all of one mind here' she said solemnly, looking down at Erin.

'The spiders killed three of our brothers' grunted a hairy troll with bristling angry eyebrows and a hint of doom in his voice.

'They captured our brother and we haven't seen him since' whispered a pretty doll wearing a sailor suit.

'And I have lost all of our people except for my two sisters here' said Anyiko, adding, 'It has to stop now.'

'What about the clowns?' asked Erin, looking over her shoulder at them. They turned to face her.

'We are not sure, but we feel we must do something' said the one who had spoken to her earlier. 'Stephane must be avenged.'

So saying, some of the group dragged cushions across and they formed a large circle, so that everyone could sit down. The fairies were the tallest of all of the rebels, although the hairy trolls looked very fierce. Erin wondered what the dolls and clowns could do, but she said nothing as she sat down, hitching her sword behind her on its belt.

'If everyone is ok, I will lead the discussion' said Anyiko looking around the group. There were grunts of assent and nodded heads. 'Erin has been

brought here, as we know, Kurtees arranged it, believing that it would serve his evil purpose.' There were nods from the group.
'But I believe that it can serve our purpose too.' she added. The others stayed silent, allowing the fairy to continue. 'Erin has a weapon that can slay Kurtees; and as we know from bitter experience, only someone from her world can kill the monster; so it is our job to arrange matters so that she can.'

'How?' asked a doll.

'We must attack the spiders in their lair under the bed' answered Anyiko. At this the trolls grunted in assent, nodding their shaggy heads vigorously, but some of the others looked dismayed.

'We will die' one of the dolls stated flatly.

'So will they' answered a troll glancing at the doll. Anyiko sighed and added sadly,

'We may die, but if we do nothing then we will die anyway.'

'The girl is too small, she will fail' one of the clowns piped up. Anyiko put a reassuring hand on Erin's shoulder and responded:

'She will not fail, for we will do this together. I will protect her with my life if I can.'

This seemed to reassure everyone, and they went on to discuss the battle plan.

'I have already sent messengers to all who we can count as friends.' announced Anyiko. 'They will assemble on this side of the swamp, staying just inside the edge of the swamp to hide from the spiders. The fairies will carry the clowns down to the edge of the swamp, the trolls and dolls can climb down of course. Once down, we will join up with all our other friends and make our way through the swamp carefully and wait right at the far edge, the one closest to the dark under the bed.'

'Who else is coming?' asked a doll.

'The Dolly Sisters are coming, as well as Handy, and the china animals. They will hide in the swamp until you arrive. The clowns can ride on Handy through the swamp; it is not a place where you can easily bounce. When all is ready, the Dolly Sisters will signal with a torch. Then everyone will advance and take the spiders on. The china animals are not strong but they are quick, they will advance in front to find the spiders and lure them in. The trolls will take up the middle position with their clubs, the dolls spread out on the flanks with their spears and the clowns stay behind them with their bows and arrows. When the spiders come, the trolls must attack them frontally, the dolls close in from the side while the clowns shoot at anything that is a threat. While all that is going on, the Dolly Sisters will signal again and the fairies with Erin will fly down and get behind the spiders, attacking Kurtees directly and then getting at the spiders from behind.'

Erin spoke up at this point.

'How will I kill this Kurtees? Surely he is much stronger than me.'

'You will have me and the fairies with you' smiled Anyiko. 'We will attack him from the air and while he is distracted, you must dash in and slay him.'

Now as a plan it seemed to Erin to be quite vague and totally dependent on the spiders doing what the rebels expected them to do. She had the feeling that Kurtees would defend himself in a much more clever way than simply send his spiders in and leave himself undefended.

'We have little choice child' Anyiko added. 'We must take them on, if they catch us in the open plain they will run around us and take us down one by one. If we stay in hiding, the same will happen. Under the bed there is less room, and the diversion of a frontal attack will distract them. Kurtees is powerful, but he can't fly. We will carry nets to trap him and make your job easier.'

'But what if we lose?' asked Erin anxiously.

'We must not lose' replied a fairy.

'Trolls will not lose' grunted the trolls.

'Good' said Anyiko firmly and stood up. 'Then it is agreed. Our friends are already making their way to the swamp through the mountains, so we must set off now. Gather your weapons.'

So they all gathered their weapons in silence, checking them before slipping out of the hatchway and crawling out onto the bookcase top. The trolls and dolls immediately swung themselves over the edge and headed down. The fairies, including Anyiko grabbed a clown each and flew off into the dark, also heading downwards, and Erin was left alone. She started suddenly as she felt something nudge her leg and looked down to see the giant lizard, which settled down in front of her as if on guard.

'Oh well, at least you are here to keep me company' she said, and the lizard turned to look at her briefly and then looked away, vigilant for any sign of an enemy.

Soon, with a whirring of wings, the fairies were back. Anyiko landed beside her and took her hand.

'Now we wait for the signal' she said, and together they stared into the gloom and hoped that all would go well.

They all waited in silence, standing close to the edge of the shelf and hoping to see a bright light, the signal that the plan was working and the fairies with Erin could fly down and complete the job. 'It will take them a while to get into position' explained Anyiko. 'So we must be patient. But while you are waiting, tell me about your world.'

So Erin told her about a world where the light was brighter. She explained about her family, her parents and her brother. She loved them all, and she spoke wistfully about them, how she enjoyed playing with Ethan her brother, how she annoyed him, made him angry, teased him and yet depended on him so much for his strength and quiet support.

She talked of their small house, littered with toys, and her tiny bedroom that she shared with Ethan. As she spoke, she could see all of her world in her mind, and she longed to be there. Then she talked about her grandparents and their house, with its rambling garden full of adventure, its fish ponds and flowers. She loved her grandparents too, her grandma was always ready to play and join in noisily, usually with a jolly laugh, fag in her mouth and beer bottle in hand. Then there was grandpa, quite and solemn at times, but who scared her deliriously into excitement when he pretended to be a dog and would chase her around the floor, barking loudly and threatening to bite her.

And then there was Auntie Lizzie. Jolly, kind and caring, who would make cakes with Erin and Ethan, and who had the mysterious bedroom with its messy floor.

It all seemed so vivid, but in some way so remote from where she was. Eventually, she ran out of things to say. Anyiko sighed and stared into the darkness and said:

'It sounds lovely, but I expect there is no place for fairies or talking toys.'

'No' replied Erin, 'I am afraid not. People would try to catch you and put you in a zoo.' Anyiko laughed.

'It may seem dark and terrible here, but it was not always this way' Anyiko explained. 'All we seemed to do was just live and be together. Not that everything was perfect, we had our problems. The spiders were always dangerous of course, but much less so than now, they would fight amongst themselves a lot as well as annoy us. The trolls can be a bit of a pest, the clowns are surprisingly unhappy and antisocial, and the dolls are a bit whiney. But we were ok, until Kurtees arrived. So here we are, waiting to die, maybe.' She paused for a second.

Erin looked up at her and said quietly:

'We won't die, we will win and then things will go back to the way they should be.'

'Yes.' replied Anyiko. 'They will.' And they fell silent again.

The waiting seemed to last for ages. Erin was hungry, and a little thirsty, but she said nothing. There was an odd silence around them, except for the occasional movement of the fairies wings and the lizard's tongue flickering in and out.

Then in the far distance, a small light sprang out and seemed to be moving from side to side as if it was being waved.

'The signal!' cried the fairies. Anyiko grabbed Erin, holding her tight to her chest and the fairies sprang into the air with a thunder of pounding wings before diving downwards. As they dived downwards, Erin felt like she had left her stomach behind, the wind rushed through her hair and buffeted her face. As they swept over the white shapes of the swamp, the fairies uttered a battle cry and Erin joined in, much to her surprise, although she didn't dare try and draw her sword in case she dropped it, so she hugged it tight to her chest.

When they were nearly at the far edge of the swamp, Erin could see that the light was much closer, although not moving, it still shone out brightly. She could hear shouting and a lot of noise she didn't recognise far ahead and the fairies swooped lower, zooming across the swamp at breakneck speed.

But then they stopped suddenly, the jerk almost dislodging her from Anyiko's grasp.

'Something is wrong!' shouted the fairy, and they stopped in the air, wings flapping swiftly as they hovered. Then the light came towards them and they gasped as they saw that it was a torch, being held up by a spider, and suddenly there were spiders everywhere, both below them and leaping up at them, trailing web strands that they were whipping through the air.

In a split second, one of the fairies was down, pulled down by strands that had whipped around it. Anyiko reacted the quickest and shot up in the air, turning to head back. Erin saw another fairy pulled down, but Anyiko had turned away and was now heading back, wings thundering as she sped above the swamp.

'We are lost' cried Anyiko in despair as she flew. Erin felt as if a lump of lead had got stuck in her stomach, she felt sad for all her new friends who had obviously been beaten in battle, or ambushed. But at least she was OK, and so was Anyiko.

Just as she thought this, Anyiko stopped dead in mid flight and Erin was jerked tumbling from her grasp. Before she had time to shout, scream or even panic, she crashed into the soft white slushiness of the swamp. She rolled over and over, luckily the swamp was soft, so she didn't break anything, but as she fell and rolled, she glimpsed the fairy with a spider strand around her ankle being hauled backwards into the dark.

Heart thumping in her chest, as she rolled to a stop she lay still, terrified for her friends and so afraid for herself. Not for the first time she thought of her family and wondered if she would ever see them again.

The shouts and scuffles seemed to be receding in the dark, and silence was slowly creeping back. The danger was not over though, for Erin guessed that spiders would be out in the swamp looking for her. So she turned, and hunching over, began to make her way back as quietly as she could towards the edge of the swamp and away from danger.

The swamp was a very odd place indeed, it was rather like trying to walk across rubbery mushy snow, and indeed the damp tissue wasn't lying totally flat, it was in clumps about as high as her in places. But above all else it was white, and Erin knew that she would stand out a mile off against the white background.

She hunched even lower and pressed on across the damp, soft ground. She could hear vague sounds in the distance and a sort of soft rustling, in her imagination she thought of spiders sneaking through the swamp looking for her, and the thought added speed to her tired legs as she pushed onwards.

Eventually the swamp became patchy white islands sitting on the carpet that she could dodge around, so now she ran as fast as she could zipping around the white islands, panting and gasping for breath as she fled. And as she ran round a large white island, she ran slap into a spider, crashing into it and they both rolled over in a flailing mass of arms and legs.

Gasping heavily, she heaved herself to her feet; the spider had already turned and was facing her, jaws twitching. Frantically she ripped the sword from her scabbard and swung it as the spider leapt hissing to the attack. It sliced clean through a leg that fell twitching to the floor.

Angry, upset and terrified, the girl advanced towards the spider that had begun to retreat and swung the sword again, this time it sliced across the mouth of the spider, opening a deep gash that had it wildly pawing and hissing at the pain. As the spider reared up she jumped forward herself and thrust the sword right through the spider's body. She heard a voice shouting in triumph, and to her surprise she realised it was hers.

The spider pulled away from her and quivered in pain before lying still, and Erin knew that it was dead. In a sudden surge all her fear and tiredness seemed to rush through her, and she fell to her knees, head spinning and stomach churning, her breath coming in great rasping gasps. As she kneeled there panting, and feeling as if her stomach was about to empty itself, she looked up at the dead spider in front of her, and the sight of it filled her with a strength and determination that surprised her, and she staggered to her feet, sword in hand.

But it is no good being strong and determined if you are on your own and being hunted down by a seemingly invincible foe. She was past the edge of the swamp now, the mountains to her right, and her instinct was to climb up and hide. She didn't know what else to do or where else to go, and she felt that if she hid too close to the swamp, the spiders would find her as they searched. So, sheathing her sword she turned towards the mountains and reaching them, began to climb them once more.

It did feel safer once she had gone a little way, she wasn't so conspicuous against the dark colours of the clothing, and she knew she could hide in folds and sleeves if she had to, so as she climbed she kept an eye open for any hiding places around her in case they were needed.

But it was very tough going for her. She was very tired, thirsty and the adrenaline from the fight had gone, leaving her shaky and weak. After she had gone as far as she could, she knew that she could go no further, so she found a nice deep fold, crawled in and fell into an exhausted sleep.
She wasn't sure how long she had been asleep, but she fuzzily came awake because in her dreams she

had been dreaming of a fluttering bird, and it was just that sound of beating wings that had woken her. Rubbing the tiredness from her eyes, she very carefully crawled up so she could see out.

It seemed a little lighter now, unless her eyes had got used to the gloom. At all events, she soon saw a fairy that was hovering and circling the mountains. Her heart jumped at the sight but she still knew she had to be careful, so looking around, she emerged from hiding and started to wave her arms, she daren't call out.

The fairy saw her and slowly flew nearer. To Erin's joy it was Anyiko, and as she landed next to Erin, the girl rushed to her and they hugged, both of them sobbing quietly but glad to be back together.

'What happened?' asked Erin through her tears. Erin could see that Anyiko's wings looked damaged and were torn in places, and she had nasty bruises on her arms and legs, including a mark that looked like a red raw burn on her ankle.

'I don't know' replied the fairy and added softly, 'It seems as if they knew we were coming. I didn't see what was going on anywhere else, but there were spiders everywhere, and the battle was just a running series of fights in isolated groups, mostly spiders running down our people and trapping them. I think some of us may have escaped, I saw some running under the bed and towards the mountains, but not on this side, they would have been heading for the darker side of the mountains that run under the bed.'

Erin looked up at Anyiko and took the fairy's hands in hers. In a soft voice, staring ahead of her, she told Anyiko of her fight with the spider, how angry she had been, how determined, and how it seemed that she had been in total control of herself, despite her fear. The only thought in her head had been that she had to kill the spider.

Anyiko smiled as Erin talked and said: 'You are telling me to buck up and be stronger little one.' Erin opened her mouth to protest, but the fairy interrupted her.

'You are right of course. We must go on, across the top of the mountains and down into the other side. It may be safer and we might also find our friends, if any have escaped.'

'We can fly of course' said Anyiko, 'but it will be very dark on the other side, so I may have to land some way up the mountain and we climb down.' And then she added, looking at Erin, 'Are you ready for this?'

Erin nodded, and once again she was in the arms of the fairy as they rose upwards.

They reached the top quite quickly, and even though there was very little space between the top of the dirty clothes mountain and the bed, they flew down the other side. But it was dark and inky black. So the fairy landed some way down the mountain, and they carefully started to descend on foot into the blackness.

So they carefully made their way downwards, sometimes having to go back up again to avoid deep crevasses. As they approached what felt like the bottom of the mountains, Anyiko suddenly put out a hand and stopped Erin. They both stood frozen in silence, at first Erin couldn't hear anything, but then, right at the edge of her hearing she could detect a faint or soft breathing sound. It didn't appear to be coming from anywhere in particular, and the two looked at each other in puzzlement.

Without warning, the mountain floor under their feet suddenly heaved up and Erin just glimpsed arms and a flash of a face that leapt upon them both and they went down in a tangle of limbs.

'Stop! Stop!' cried Anyiko and the mystery assailant drew back. Erin looked up in alarm from where she lay and she saw that it was Yvonna.

'Thank God' Yvonna breathed and they all got up, dusting themselves down. Anyiko was about to ask what was happening, but Yvonna put a finger to her lips in the gloom and gestured them to follow.

They soon came up to a fold in the cloth and Yvonna squeezed inside. They followed her and clambered through some tight nooks and crannies, pushing through some folds and clambering up others. They came to a sleeve opening and Yvonna crawled in, and the others followed. The sleeve was a tight space and stuffy and they had to push hard to get through, the rough woolly fabric closed in on them as they went.

Yvonna then tumbled from sight and they followed her down a dark hole that opened out into a large space. The space was dimly lit, but fairies have the power to glow, and there was a fairy there already, glowing a soft blue light that illuminated the chamber they were in, and revealed that there were others there.

Erin realised at once that they were survivors of the battle with the spiders, looking forlorn and tired; some of them seemed to be injured. There were a couple of trolls, some china animals, and of course Yvonna, the Dolly Sister.

'This is all of us that are left' declared Yvonna. The surviving rebels looked up and greeted Erin and Anyiko with downcast eyes, silent and despondent.

'What happened?' asked Anyiko as she plonked herself down on a large fold with a sigh.

'It was Sanders the clown' replied the remaining fairy. 'He lit a torch before we were ready, not to signal you but to signal the spiders. And then, they were all over us.'

'I don't believe it' Anyiko exclaimed in disbelief.

Yvonna put a comforting arm around her.

'It is true' she said. 'As the spiders attacked, he was crying and begging us to forgive him. They had captured Stephane, and told him they would kill him unless he betrayed us. He had no choice.'

'Trolls would not tell' grunted a troll gruffly.

'Perhaps not' said Yvonna, 'But that is what happened. We made it here and have so far been safe but we can't stay here.'

So there they were, hiding in a space under the clothes mountain, and seemingly nowhere to go. Erin looked around at the small group that was left and they all looked exhausted. She felt just as disconsolate as the others, and couldn't believe that things could get worse. Aware that the spiders would be looking for them, the fairy that had been glowing let her light slowly fade, so that they were all in complete darkness

Outside, the hunt for the survivors was obviously on, Erin could faintly hear the pattering of spider feet across the ground and over the mountain around them. The most disconcerting feeling though was when a spider would run overhead, because the fabric above them would dip slightly with the pressure of their feet. It felt almost as if the spiders were feeling for them, and at these moments, everyone would be as still and silent as statues.

So there they all lay, in the darkness, silent as graves, entombed in the depth of the mountain, waiting and praying for search to go away. Erin didn't really know how long they waited, but eventually all sounds of movement outside seemed to fade away and silence fell.

'I will risk a light' whispered Anyiko; she began to glow faintly, revealing the frightened faces of her companions and the dark folds of their hideaway.

But then there came a new sound, faint in the distance, but quite odd, and as it came closer it got odder still. It sounded like someone dragging something heavy across the ground, not hard ground, it was a sort of squishy sound, a bit like dragging a sack of potatoes through a puddle, and it was getting louder and louder.

Everyone stood up, grasping what weapons they had, looking all around uncertainly, unsure what was happening. Around them the folds of cloth were moving and swaying, when suddenly something burst into the group and a chorus of shouts and screams broke out.

There was a flash of bright light as the two fairies lit up their glows fully to illuminate the scene. What Erin saw was a scene almost from an old horror film. For in their midst was a huge slug, at least as long as the fairies were tall, and a transparent green colour, with eyes swaying on long stalks. It had slid in from inside the folds of cloth somewhere, and landed on top of where the animals were lying. It was covered with a sticky yellowish slime that suddenly seemed to be everywhere, and it stank of rotting vegetables. Erin had never before been so close to being sick. More horrible to behold though was that the slug had obviously landed right on top of the few china animals and somehow already absorbed them inside it, Erin could dimly see them floating there and not moving.

Pandemonium had broken out, everyone in the tiny space was trying to attack was the slug, the trolls whacking it with their clubs and the elves with their spears, but the weapons seemed to bounce off its rubbery surface. The slug itself was whipping its eye stalks around, and sliding deceptively quickly towards Erin.

Quick as thought, Erin whipped out her sword and slashed at the eye stalks, severing them completely. The slug writhed in pain, knocking some of its attackers of their feet, and turning, it vanished quickly, sliding up into a fold and making its escape.

The group of rebels stood there panting, weapons in hand and draped in sticky tendrils of smelly goo and looking at each other.

'What on earth was that?' panted Erin.

'A giant slug' replied Anyiko, 'they normally live way under the bed, right at the back. I never expected to see one here. But well done little Erin, I fear we would have lost more people if you had not done what you did.'

The others murmured approvingly, even the trolls were impressed and patted her on the head with heavy hands.

'But what happened to the poor animals?' asked Erin. Yvonna answered her.

'I'm afraid the animals are lost, the slug sucked them up into its stomach.'

'Then we are lost too.' Erin replied sadly. 'There are so many monsters here, how can we hope to survive even to escape, much less actually kill this Kurtees spider.'

The others couldn't really answer. She added in a soft and hopeless voice: 'We will all end up like the animals, sucked up into some creatures' stomach.' Anyiko and Yvonna put reassuring arms around her, but it made no difference to her mood.

'Sucked up into a stomach' she whispered, and then, paused... and a smile slowly started to move across her face.
'Sucked into a stomach!' she shouted, and the others shushed her, wondering what on earth had come over her. But all their shushing had no effect, and she danced around with a huge grin on her face singing "Sucked up into a stomach!" over and over again.

But then she calmed down, and in a lower voice asked: 'Can Handy be killed by the spiders?'
The others thought for a minute and Anyiko replied,

'Probably not, I suppose they could tie him up with their strands, but then Handy can't do much to them, even if he swallows them, they won't die. After all, he swallowed you.'

'Exactly' smiled Erin, and added, 'I have a plan', and told them of her idea in swift whispers.

'It might work' breathed Yvonna.

'It will work' said Erin, 'now who is going to go?'

'I will' replied the other fairy, and she pushed her way through the folds and was gone.

'While she has gone, let us prepare our weapons and finalise the plan,' Erin announced to the group, and that is what they did.

A heaving and tossing of fabric around their hideaway signalled the return of the fairy and Handy, whose huge face pushed in and smiled broadly when he saw Erin.

'Little Erin' he boomed, and added with a slightly quizzical look 'Hmm... maybe not so little Erin.' Erin was overjoyed to see him, and hugged his large long sock body as best as she could. Swiftly she explained the plan to Handy.

'I cannot take you all' he said looking round, 'but I will take who I can'

'Can you take everyone except the fairies?' asked Erin.

'Yes I think so' Handy replied.

'Ok, let's do it' said Erin.

A few minutes later, Handy, with two fairies hovering in the air above him, emerged from a fold in the mountains and slithered down to the floor level. Anyone observing him would have thought they were watching a giant multi-coloured snake that had just swallowed a very oddly shaped meal, although they would have been puzzled at the sound of the sock monsters stomach apparently talking to itself.

'Me squashed' said a low grumpy voice.

'Shhh!' exclaimed another.

'No shush troll unless you want thick ear.' Anyiko, hovering above hissed,

'Be quiet you lot!'

Erin, inside the sock monster, squashed in with her friends wondered if this was what it was like when people said they had eaten something that disagreed with them.

So they journeyed on, hugging the mountains on one side and with the blackness in front and on the other side. The fairies were carrying bows and spears slung across their backs, and these were put to use when they flew up and ahead suddenly. Then they returned, and Handy passed the bodies of three spiders, shot from the air. This was repeated a couple of times, the fairies acting as forward scouts and still the odd trio pressed onwards.

When the mountains eventually gave way to swamp on their right, the fairies turned to the left and headed for the deepest patch of darkness. It now was truly pitch black, and the fairies dared not fly, somewhere above them was the base of the bed, and they didn't want to get tangled in anything up there. They didn't dare show a light either, so they all pressed on, navigating by instinct more than anything else.

But soon they stopped, for they could hear a pattering of spider feet, not just one or two, but what sounded like hundreds, coming towards them from all sides.

'We are surrounded.' whispered Yvonna.

'Form a circle!' commanded Anyiko, and they did, forming a circle facing outwards, with Handy in the middle, weapons at the ready.

When the attack came, it was swift and devastating. A horde of spiders charged from all sides, scuttling across the floor and leaping in the air. The spiders knocked the defenders over, or trapped them in web strands, it was so swift and deadly that the defenders had no chance to even fight back properly, and soon they were all down, except for Handy, who was curled up in the middle of the circle of trussed defenders.

Then it got darker and colder, and a huge misty black shape approached them, it had a head of glittering black eyes, with jaws that dripped venom that hissed as it struck the ground. It had long taloned legs that emerged somehow from the dense misty centre, and a wicked black sting dragged across the ground behind it. It hissed with gloating laughter as it approached.

'Foolisssh creatures' it hissed in gloating triumph, 'I led you here, I let you kill my people, and on you came, hoping for successs, but now it is I, Kurteessss who has triumphed.'

The spider picked its way through the trussed up rebels, prodding them with its claws as it went, the other spiders withdrew a little as if in terror. Each time it prodded a helpless figure, it hissed with satisfaction.

Then it reached Handy. 'Ah, our ssssilly ssssock monsssster. Now it isss your turn.'
Handy lifted his head.

‘You can’t kill Handy mister spider.’ he said in defiance.

‘Oh yesss I can!’ and with that the monster leapt upon Handy and pinned him down with its claws. ‘My sssting will dissssolve your ssspirit ssso I can drink it in!’ it boasted in triumph and raised itself up in the air to strike.

‘Oh no it won’t’ cried a girls voice, and with a swift tearing noise, a long blade shot upwards from inside Handy and pierced the spider right through the dark mist in its centre.

The spider screamed in pain and fury, and through the slit she had cut in Handy's body, Erin emerged, still holding the sword with both hands.

She twisted and turned it inside the spider, which writhed with flailing legs, falling onto its back, hissing and cursing with Erin holding on to the sword grimly, ignoring the spiders legs rasping against her.

Kurtees heaved himself to his feet, and Erin rolled out from underneath him, pulling the sword free, black blood gushing from the awful wound onto the floor.

It was a horrible sight as the spider convulsed in pain, but seizing the opportunity, Erin stepped right in front of it and plunged the sword in again, right into the middle of its eyes, forcing the blade in as far as she could, and with a final spasm and a flood of dark blood, the spider died.

As she stood there, panting and gasping with exertion, she looked down at the spider and watched as it just seemed to revert to the black slime from where it had come, and a dark puddle spread across the floor. She dashed over to Handy, jumping on him and hugging him tightly.

'Are you ok' she asked.

'Of course' he replied. 'Handy just made of sock, easy to sew up hole.'

The spiders meanwhile seeing the demise of their leader, and perhaps losing the spell of his command, dashed away in fear and vanished into the darkness.

It even seemed to be getting lighter now. Maybe, thought Erin, Kurtees was causing the darkness, so now it is looking just like a room again.

So she took her sword and freed all her friends from their bonds, who greeted her joyously. Yvonna hugged her tight and Anyiko solemnly praised her.

'You have freed this world of a great evil, we will forever be in your debt.' she said. As the gloom departed, they all noticed what looked like a group of people in the distance, so they ran across to them, as they ran they could see that there were indeed a lot of people there of all shapes, sizes and types, all trussed up in spider bonds.

Here, Erin's sword came in handy again, and she moved from person to person, freeing them all. Now there really was a party going on, with trolls, clowns, fairies, dolls, animals and one bouncing sock monster all dancing with joy and greeting each other.

Even the Dolly Sisters were there, trussed up, their lovely lace clothes all disarranged and torn. As Erin freed each one, they hugged her tightly, speechless and tearful.

One of the last ones she freed was Stephane, who greeted her with tears of joy running down his face, so happy he couldn't speak but just kept squeezing her in a monster hug.

Anyiko came over to her then and said:

'Child, we must get you to the door, or it will close.' So she picked Erin up, and they flew away, Erin waving to all her friends below, who waved back, calling out their thanks.

Anyiko kept low, skimming across the floor and they came to where one wall joined the other, and right at the join was a shining door shape, about Erin's size.

'Quickly child!' commanded the fairy as she landed, and Erin, jumping off, began to run, but turned back suddenly and hugged her friend.

‘You did well Erin’, the fairy said ‘But take care, you were bitten by a spider to get here, I don’t know if that means anything, but please take care.’
Erin looked up at the fairy.

‘Thank you’ she said simply and ran towards the door. She wasn’t sure what to do when she got there, it was just a shimmering door shape, so she stepped through, and was suddenly back in the real Auntie Lizzie’s bedroom.

There was the bookcase, the glass penguin standing silently on it, the pile of dirty clothes, the used tissues. But all of it was silent and still.

She looked down at her hands and her clothes, everything seemed normal, and she felt just as she had felt before her adventure started. Perhaps inside a little older and wiser.

But she could hear her brother playing outside, and her grandma laughing. It was daylight, the birds were singing, the sun was shining, and so Erin ran downstairs and out in the garden to play.

49780630R00090

Made in the USA
Charleston, SC
04 December 2015